ANGELA D. SHELTON

Independence

Collapse Book Three

To those who have been set free, I dedicate this novel.

Contents

1

Chapter One

"No, Dad. Don't leave. We can find another way." At just seventeen years of age, Olivia Jackson faced a world falling apart—again. How much sorrow was one person expected to shoulder? Wasn't it enough that she lost her mother?

Her father's expressionless face hurt her more than if he'd shown some anger. "There's no other way. I'm sorry. I can't add another mouth to feed to my brother's home."

Uncle Kevin and Aunt Amanda stood behind Olivia, facing her retreating father.

Uncle Kevin reiterated the same offer he'd made dozens of times in the last twenty-four hours. "Tom, you don't need to do this. We'll make it work."

Aunt Amanda rubbed Olivia's shoulders from behind. "Come on, Tom. Your brother's right. There's no need to split your family apart."

Dad whirled back to them, his eyes blazing. The hands he'd been wringing now jammed in his pockets, his resolve hardening. "Once I find work, I'll come back and get you. I won't have my baby sleeping on the streets. It's not safe."

"Take Olivia inside, Amanda." Uncle Kevin waved toward the door. "My brother and I need to talk."

"No!" Olivia couldn't let her father out of her sight. "I need to stay with Dad."

Her uncle's glare revealed his anger. "Amanda. Now."

Aunt Amanda pulled at Olivia's arm, steering her away.

Olivia shouted over her shoulder as she allowed herself to be drawn back toward the house. "Promise me you won't leave without saying goodbye!"

No response came from her father, and she dissolved into sobs. Aunt Amanda folded Olivia into her arms as they trudged away.

«»

It was dark outside when Olivia woke, lying atop the bedspread. Dried tears glued her eyelids shut, and a heaviness pressed her into the bed.

Though no one had told her as much, she knew her father was gone. Aunt Amanda stopped by the room multiple times, offering water, soup, a hug, anything to help ease the pain and loneliness. But the lump that settled in Olivia's chest threatened to heave up anything left in her stomach from breakfast.

When she rolled to her side, the soggy pillowcase cooled her cheek.

Now what? Not only was her mother gone, but her father as well. Abandoned. Stranded with an extended family she barely knew.

Uncle Kevin brought his family to Columbus last year, and they stayed with Olivia and her father for a few short months, trying to find work. Dad thought he could get Uncle Kevin a job at the factory. Instead, Dad lost *his* position.

They didn't stay long after that. Dad's drinking drove them away.

She got out of bed and wandered down the hallway to the bathroom. There was no electricity tonight. Power was never a guarantee these days. Tonight, a full moon shone through the bathroom window. With the door open, it lit the hallway enough to keep her from stubbing her toes.

After using the toilet, she rinsed her hands under the faucet. There wasn't any soap. She hadn't seen soap regularly since her father lost his job, and it had been sparse before that.

Funny how she used to take minor items like hygiene for granted. Mom had been so picky about her laundry detergent. She had to have a particular scent and would stop at two or three stores if they were out of what she liked.

That was *before.* Before the variant. Before it all fell apart. Before Mom died.

Olivia dried her hands on a rough towel, inhaling a scent she wasn't expecting—vinegar. Interesting. People made do with what they had, but she'd never heard of washing laundry with vinegar. Couldn't be worse than nothing at all, though, right?

She gazed into the mirror. Though her long brunette hair looked black in the dark, her swollen eyes provided a dead giveaway to a long night of tears.

As she padded back up the hallway, she passed by her cousin's room. Mumbling came from inside as if Rob were having nightmares. They all had their demons now. *She* certainly did.

Back in her room, she slipped under the covers. The night had turned chilly, so she pulled up an extra blanket from the bottom of the bed. Even with no heat in the house, it only got cool late into the evening and early the next day. Of course, there was no air conditioning either, and the Georgia heat was harder to hide from than the cold.

Snuggling under the covers, she let her mind drift. Was there a chance she could fall asleep again? Perhaps staying awake was better anyway. She didn't want to wake up to life without her father.

Dad wouldn't be back. She didn't know how she knew, but her brain resolved it. She should be grateful he'd stopped drinking long enough to bring her to Shiloh. He'd only remain sober if he ran out of alcohol. But somehow, even when he couldn't earn a dime for a meal, he always found a way to get a drink.

If only he'd put as much time and attention into finding work. She might still have a family.

Enough!

Tomorrow, she had to face her new life. She had to make it without him now or find someone else to take care of her. Maybe Aunt Amanda and Uncle Kevin meant what they said. Perhaps they would be her caregivers.

She drifted off to sleep with the crickets chirping outside her window and her cousin mumbling nightmares in the room next door.

«»

Three months later…

"Olivia, can you please come help me?" Aunt Amanda hollered from outside the open bedroom window. "I've got the net all tangled up and can't get this bird free."

Still dressing for the day, Olivia looked out the screen and groaned. What a tangled mess her aunt had gotten into!

"I'll be right there."

She picked up her jacket and slid her arms into it. A little nippy this morning, today promised some relief from the previous day's heat. Fall eased out the oppressive summer temps but brought worries of how they would survive after the growing season.

As she opened her bedroom door, her uncle's voice emanated from the kitchen. From the low tones, he must want the conversation to remain private, so he was discussing her cousin or lecturing Rob in person.

Either way, she'd rather avoid the discussion. She quickened her pace toward the front door.

Her stomach growled. Their hard work in the garden produced limited success. Before they'd found a barrier, the deer ate every bean they planted. The second planting produced only anemically. Nothing like the Worthingtons' garden next door.

As Olivia rounded the side of the house, Aunt Amanda's brow furrowed, and her lips pressed tight. "I don't know how I got this so tangled up. I think the bird is in worse shape than when I started."

The six-foot-tall net fence kept deer out. The barrier ran around the perimeter of their plot, tacked up to poles on the four corners. A dove flapped its wings, tangled in the material.

Olivia hustled over. "I guess adding the top section to keep birds out worked. Maybe a little too well."

The fowl's frantic movements stopped as her aunt grasped it and folded its wings by its sides. A trickle of blood emanated from the tousled feathers, and Olivia cringed. She hated to see any animal suffering. Even if it was stealing their food. Sections of mesh crisscrossed its body in a hopeless tangle. "Should I get a knife or some scissors? I'm not sure how else to get it out."

Her aunt shook her head. "We can't waste the material. It took us months to find this, and who knows if we'd find a replacement if we hack it up." A long sigh escaped her lips. "We may not save the bird. That's what it gets for trying to steal our sunflowers."

Like the trapped bird, Olivia's heart fluttered in her chest. Letting the bird die was more than she could bear. "Let me try."

Her thin fingers lifted the bird's wing, causing more flutters and cheeps. The mesh cut deep into its joint, and its feathers pulled in awkward directions.

"Come on, little one. We're trying to save you, but you need to help yourself and stay calm," Aunt Amanda cooed.

Once more, Olivia touched the tiny body and worked one square of the net off the wing, then smoothed the feathers into place. "One down. Quite a few to go."

With a sigh, her aunt nodded for her to continue.

Little by little and section by section, they spent the next half hour freeing the bird. By the time they removed the net from its feet, all three shook from strained muscles.

"Moment of truth." Aunt Amanda lowered the dove to the ground. "Let's see if you can still fly."

They released it, and the bird flew a few feet, then dropped back onto the grass.

Olivia walked toward it, but before she could get within arm's reach, it flew up again and landed in a nearby oak tree. "Good enough. At least in a tree, it won't be lunch. If it's lucky, it'll get over the shock and find its way home."

Planting her hands on her hips, she faced the net. Perhaps they could salvage it. The bird's gyrations and their efforts to free it had broken some strands.

From the house, her uncle shouted, "If you live under this roof, you'll do what I say! Otherwise, you can get out."

Aunt Amanda winced and brushed her grimy hands on her jeans. "I'd better go see if I can help."

"I'll stay here and work on this." Olivia knew better than to go inside now. "It'll take most of the morning to figure this tangle out. Good thing I like puzzles."

She smiled at her aunt to ease her burdens and received a weak grin in return. In this house, joy was scarce as food, and laughter as nonexistent as soap.

After Aunt Amanda returned to the house, a calm came over the building. At least Olivia couldn't hear anything from outside. Quiet was the most she could ask for.

Rob was a hot mess. He was lucky the prisons barely functioned these days and could only hold the most hardened criminals. Many states reinstated the death penalty for heinous crimes to keep the worst off the streets.

Her cousin wasn't dangerous. Just an alcoholic.

While Rob's recent history with a deceptive criminal added to his problems, her father was likely to blame for Rob's alcohol addiction. She wished they'd never gotten together.

Her fingers continued to unravel the knots. A rumble in her gut reminded her she'd not eaten yet. If Rob would stop drinking, perhaps the family could focus on their food situation.

Aunt Amanda didn't want to push him to go cold turkey. A local doctor advised them a sudden stop could kill him. The physician had connections to an Atlanta specialist with access to the medications to wean Rob off alcohol. But they had to wait for the drugs to arrive via courier, and that didn't happen often these days.

She arched her back and tried to stretch out the spasms in her hands. There was so much to miss from her old life. How had she not appreciated the conveniences of the daily mail, Amazon two-day shipping, and even pizza delivery?

But more than anything, she missed her parents.

Labor Day had to be coming up soon, but there wouldn't be any picnic.

Halloween would be next, and if her mom was still alive, they'd be planning some silly costumes.

When Thanksgiving came, Mom cooked the best turkey dinner. Closing her eyes, Olivia could almost smell the savory gravy simmering on the stove, the spicy apple pie baking in the oven, and the dressing crisping to accompany the main course.

All gone.

Now she lived with a family she struggled to understand and endured their daily battle. Rob wasn't the only one who dealt with his drinking. The whole family lived it.

That struggle was on top of the need to work for every morsel of food they put on the table.

The net slowly became untangled under her fingertips. Unloop here and uncross there, stretch it out and reattach to the poles. A snail's pace, but she had nothing else to do, much less anyone to talk to. Because of her petite five-foot frame, she needed a cinder block to reach the tops of the poles, but she'd learned to be resourceful in the years since the supply chain collapsed.

When a day started like today, no one would pay attention to her. Rob's problem would absorb her aunt and uncle until he fell into bed that evening. That was a given.

If only she could visit her former friend, Jan, on their farm up the road. In the month since Rob admitted to helping blackmail Jan's brother, none of them had gone to the Worthington ranch. Though Jan's brother forbade Rob access to the farm, the other family would never forbid her contact. But embarrassment kept them apart.

How do you tell someone you're sorry your cousin extorted them to get what they had?

She missed Jan. She missed the farm. She missed Caleb. And her body missed the food they used to enjoy when they ate their communal meals.

Now she'd spend her day untangling this net to protect a sad excuse for a garden. Though Jan and her family had been teaching her how to grow food, she had so much more to learn. The jaundiced-looking produce proved it.

Why couldn't they all reconcile?

Her stomach rumbled.

A tear slipped down her cheek, and she swiped it away. How could Rob ruin everything? How could she fix it? And how long could she live like this?

She tightened her fists. Her ragged nails cut into her palms as her breathing quickened. She couldn't bring her dad back. But, surely, she could find her way in life again. Find someone to care about her and take care of her. Find a place she belonged without the pall this family cast over her.

2

Chapter Two

Olivia's back cramped, and her muscles burned, begging her to stop working her end of the two-man saw. But after one look at Aunt Amanda's determined face, flushed and dripping with sweat, Olivia couldn't stop yet.

The felled tree lay between them, and they'd made it halfway through the width of it. Once the saw broke through the bottom, they could take a break.

Push, pull, push, pull.

Wood shavings piled in front of her toes, stuck between her socks and her worn-out sneakers, and coated her dripping face.

"Hold up a second." Aunt Amanda released the saw handle, shaking her arms while she opened and closed her fingers. "Sorry. My hands are cramping so bad I couldn't hold it one more minute."

What a relief.

Olivia stretched her back, standing tall on her tiptoes, then side-to-side. Twisting at her waist, she flung her arms back and forth with each motion to get her circulation flowing again.

The crack of an ax against a tree told her where her uncle and Rob were working.

Her throat burned, reminding her to find her thermos. It better not be empty yet. How many times had she shared it back and forth with her aunt? Three? Four? The day was a blur of work with too little rest.

She collapsed on a log, pulled open her backpack, and found her backup water. A quick shake sloshed the remaining quarter of the liquid up its sides. Good thing they always brought two bottles each. Of course, Rob forgot his—typical. So, Aunt Amanda had given him hers and shared Olivia's.

If only she could find more bottles, Olivia would carry as many as would fit in her backpack. Who knew how valuable a water bottle would be after a variant wiped out millions of people's lives and took the supply chain with them? It wasn't like they could run down to the corner store and pick up a spare. How many water bottles had society tossed into the trash before it all fell apart, just because they'd gotten a newer, cuter one?

Stupid variant.

She twisted the top off and sipped enough to quench the burn in her throat. Aunt Amanda looked in the opposite direction, avoiding eye contact. Probably because she didn't want to ask for water since it was her son's fault they were short.

"Here." Olivia held the thermos out. "There's still some left."

Aunt Amanda wobbled out a weak smile. "That's okay. I'm good."

Olivia huffed out a long breath, leaving her hand extended, the water still proffered. "You don't look all right. You look like a drowned rat. Replacing fluids is important. You *don't* want us to have to carry you out of here. Personally, I don't think I could."

Her aunt mopped her face with her drenched T-shirt, smearing dirt and bits of sawdust as if she were a soldier prepping for battle with camo paint.

Olivia couldn't help it. She giggled. Aunt Amanda's confused look turned Olivia's chuckle into a belly laugh. Tears rolled down her face, competing with the sweat.

Aunt Amanda snatched the bottle, brought it to her lips, and drank. "What's so funny?"

Her scowl simply struck Olivia as hilarious, and she doubled over with uncontrolled laughter. "You should see your face."

Her aunt twisted the lid back in place, tipped the metal bottle sideways, and inspected her reflection. Her lips lifted on one side, but shouts came from where the men were working.

Olivia's laughter died after its too-brief life.

Rob stormed up the path they'd created in the woods—face dark and eyes flashing. He passed them, growling as he went. "He treats me like I'm an idiot. I don't have to put up with that."

Uncle Kevin wasn't far behind, grasping an ax. "Come back here. We've got work to do."

Rob stomped over a knoll without a backward glance. As the top of his head disappeared, he hollered back. "Do it yourself."

That was that. The end to their tenuous peace.

At least they'd gotten a few hours of work out of him before his mood shifted into the dark zone.

Once Uncle Kevin reached them, he gave up the pursuit. Resting the ax head on the ground, he leaned on it and swiped at his brow. "That boy needs his head set back on straight. One of these days, I'm going to knock some sense into him."

Aunt Amanda winced. "He worked hard today—better than

most. He's making progress."

Right. Rob had gotten out of bed, dressed himself, shared in the meager breakfast of grits, and showed up on the job. A rare day, indeed.

Still, Uncle Kevin shook his head at the path. "We all need to work as many hours as we can putting up firewood. How else are we going to get food if we don't have anything to sell?"

She was tired of the same conversation, the same question—*every* day. Was Rob going to work today? Drink today? Be part of the solution today?

She left the two of them to muddle through their familiar arguments.

Wandering down the path to where the men had been working, she found the jumbled pile of firewood. She didn't have the strength to split the logs as the men did. But her arms were stronger than they'd ever been. Manual labor will do that for a girl.

Lips pressed tight, she set to gathering the individual pieces and stacking them onto their makeshift sled. Once the sled was full, they'd take turns pulling it down the path to the house.

On market day, a truck would pick up two of them and a load of firewood. Then they'd sell it for the best price they could get. Most people didn't have money, but food was an excellent trade.

Her ponytail flopped against her chin as she bent to gather another armload. Mom used to say her hair was like satin—soft and shiny. Back then, it smelled of strawberry shampoo. Now it was full of wood chips and sweat.

She didn't like her new life. Not even a little. It stunk—big time.

《》

They'd stacked the last stick of wood on their display pile and were now ready to negotiate. Rob glowered at Olivia. So, what was new? He always looked angry.

No way would he bait her into an argument. She'd give him the choice of tasks. She wiped her forearm across her damp forehead, snugged her ball cap back on, and pulled her hair through the back. "Would you like to look for buyers? Or babysit the base?"

A sneer took over his lips. "Neither."

Heat smoldered in her chest and pulsed to her limbs as he retrieved his backpack and walked away from his responsibilities—again.

You've got to be kidding me.

If he had no intention of helping her, why had he even come today?

Easy answer. He was out of booze.

Only two of them fit in the small electric truck they bought a ride from each week. With the bed full of firewood, the only room remaining was in the tiny cab.

The truck's owner, Ryan Donahue, always helped them to load and unload. His assistance was probably more about expediency and getting the next paying customer into the truck than about kindness.

Once they'd finished their set up, one of them would walk around the outdoor market seeking people to trade. The other would man the wood and deal with customers who came to them. Without her partner, she wouldn't sell nearly as much. Their deal with Mr. Donahue ensured that any wood not sold became his. Some days, he really made out well. Today would be a good day for him.

She fisted her hands and ground her teeth against the urge

to scream her frustration at the growing crowds. Then a lump clogged her throat, and she swallowed it down rather than give in and cry. How could she be so alone in the world? What she wouldn't give to have a best friend or a boyfriend or perhaps a boyfriend who was her best friend.

"Good morning. Is the wood seasoned?"

A tall guy with sandy-blond hair smiled at her. With a well-kempt beard, he looked clean—smelled it too, without the stench of sweat most men had. Even his teeth appeared in good shape. At least she didn't see any sign of decay in his slow grin. He might be a decade older than she was, but these days, a girl needed a mature man to handle what this crazy new life threw at her.

He took care of himself. Clean clothes, clean body, and time to smile at her. That meant he had money, so she stood a decent chance of making a sale. Perhaps even gaining a new, repeat customer. No one was with him, so maybe he was unattached. She just might get more than a sale out of this transaction.

She put everything she had into her smile and gave him her full attention. "Yes, it is. We chopped this wood in the spring, so it's had all summer to dry. It'll burn hot without too much smoke." She planted her hands on her waist, cocked one hip to the side, and grinned. "How much would you like?"

"Well now, aren't you the crafty salesperson?" He winked and crossed his arms over his chest. "What if I need it delivered to my place? Can you manage that?"

Now there was a problem. She might work out a deal with Mr. Donahue to deliver the wood, but it would cost her. It needed to be worth the effort and expense. "You buy the entire load, and I'll get it delivered for you."

His left eyebrow rose. "The entire load, huh? What'll that

cost me?"

Good question. She'd never sold a full load before, but hours went into chopping the tree down, trimming off the branches, cutting the logs, splitting them into firewood, hauling it out of the woods and then to the sale. The pile of wood represented days' worth of work. And they needed food.

What if she could get more than just a few meals out of it? "I'd need a dozen laying hens and a bag of corn—or the equivalent."

His other eyebrow rose to join the first one.

After a beat of silence, he slid his hands into his jeans pockets and rocked back on his cowboy boot heels. "A dozen hens? That seems steep for a pile of firewood. Besides, I don't have any chickens to sell."

Perhaps the price was too steep for a load of wood, but he hadn't shut her down. He wanted the wood. She needed to get to the right price. "I've seen chickens at other booths. I'm certain you could arrange a trade. Or you could pay me in gold, and I could negotiate for the birds myself."

A grin slid across his lips and lifted the corners of his mouth. "You know how to bargain, don't you? Not backing down on the count, huh? A half dozen makes more sense."

Come to think of it, how was she going to get a dozen chickens home? She couldn't exactly put them in the truck cab. And no way would they all merrily ride along in the truck bed, either. She hadn't thought it all the way through.

What about the dog cage back at the house? There hadn't been a dog in the house since she'd moved in, but they must have had one before. If she brought that, she could secure the birds in it for the ride home.

Pulling on her ball cap bill, she did her best to project confidence. "Tell you what. You bring me that bag of corn now. I'll deliver the wood to your house, and you can have the chickens waiting for me to pick up when I get there. Easy-peasy."

"You drive a hard bargain, but it's probably worth it to have a pretty thing like you deliver to me in person. I wouldn't mind watching you unload a stick or two out at my place." His eyes wandered up and down her body as if he were sizing up a different purchase. "Perhaps I could even convince you to indulge in a glass of tea on the front porch after we've finished our transaction."

Oddly, the comment combined with the look he was giving her sent alarms shooting up her spine. The hair on the back of her neck stood up. Something wasn't right about this guy.

Time to end the bargaining.

"I'm certain the men who'll help me with the delivery would appreciate a drink. But it all depends on timing." That should dissuade him of any notions. "Do we have an agreement, then?"

He barked out a laugh. "We do. My name is Nick, by the way. Nick Davis. And who might you be?"

She didn't feel comfortable getting too cozy with this guy. But business was business. "Olivia."

"Well, Ms. Olivia No Last Name. Let's shake on this deal. Then I'll get you the feed."

She stuck her hand out to him, but instead of the firm shake, he grasped her fingers, turned her hand flat, and lowered his lips to kiss it.

"Until later, my dear."

He sauntered into the crowd, leaving her cheeks burning and thoughts tumbling.

What was this guy up to? Was she just being a nervous Nellie? Maybe this guy could be *the one.* Someone who could be there just for her. Someone she could be safe with.

Or maybe she should heed those warning signals.

3

Chapter Three

For the first time, Olivia set out the Sold Out sign early in the day, and with a full load of wood in front of her. Should she continue to sell wood and ask Mr. Donahue to stop back at the house to pick up a second load for delivery to Nick?

Nah. Once Rob returned, she'd leave him to babysit the pile and wander through the market. He could wait for Nick and the grain. Maybe he'd stay sober long enough to accept the down payment. If he fell asleep and missed Nick, she'd skin him alive.

The market bustled today, blissfully cool with temperatures in the upper seventies or lower eighties. Fall was a welcome respite from the blistering heat.

Boredom overtook her as she waited for her cousin. By the time he arrived, she'd dug a hole three inches deep with the toe of her shoe just to pass the time.

Rob's face told her a storm was brewing, but she sprang to her feet, ready to tangle with him. "Did you at least sell some wood while you were out there?"

His glare answered better than words could have. He pointed at her sign. "Doesn't look like I needed to. Now does it?"

He stormed past her and flopped onto an upturned log.

She ground her teeth. Pushing him would get her nowhere and make for a miserable ride home. At least he was back, so she wasn't stuck babysitting the woodpile. "We'll deliver the wood to a guy named Nick Davis. He should stop by before day's end and drop off chicken feed. Then we'll arrange with Mr. Donahue to deliver the wood and pick up a flock of chickens."

Rob just shrugged. "Whatever."

She closed her eyes. Deep breath in, hold, slow release. He wasn't going to rile her up. Eyes open again, she heard giggles.

A gaggle of children ran past, shoving each other as they laughed. A small girl tailed them, clinging to a filthy rag doll. She couldn't have been older than five. Snarled hair hung past her shoulders, too dirty to determine its correct color. A streak in the dirt on her tiny face marked the track of recent tears.

Olivia's heart ached. Seeing the little pixie brought flashbacks of life on the streets with her father. A frightening experience.

If only she could help her.

Who was she kidding? She could barely help herself as the grumbling in her stomach proved.

The woodpile forgotten, and feeling like a stalker, she followed the gang of children. Where were they headed? Little ones shouldn't be alone in the market. What happened to their parents?

Keeping up was challenging as their smaller bodies shimmied through tight spots where the queues thickened. At one point, she lost them behind a vendor selling hay bales.

Slippery little nippers, those kids.

She rounded a hay trailer and halted. There they were, surrounding a strikingly beautiful woman working at a table. A beige wide-brimmed sunhat covered the woman's head, but she pulled it off and placed it on the table as the children begged her attention.

Jars of golden liquid lined the table, and the sweet scent of honey surrounded the area. When was the last time Olivia indulged in something sweet?

The deeply tanned woman smiled and joked with the gang. She hugged each of the children as she kneeled. The dirtiest little tagalong came around the group and stroked the woman's long ebony hair.

Rather than cringing at the child's grimy hands running through her locks, the woman gathered the imp into her arms and kissed the top of her head. The child melted into her as if it was the first hug after a drought of affection. She whispered something in the girl's ear. They beamed at each other, then separated.

Who was this woman? The children obviously cared for her, as did she for them.

She stood and moved to an old picnic cooler under the shade of her table. Excited whispers ran through the group. After reaching inside, she removed a blue plastic bowl and peeled back the lid. Little heads bobbed and weaved, eager for whatever was in the container.

Once more, the woman kneeled to their level. She slid an amber candy out of the bowl and handed the piece to the first little boy.

He dropped the treat onto his tongue, and his eyes lit as he closed his lips. He backed away, sucking and rolling the sweet around in his mouth.

Each child received one piece of candy while the tiniest girl stood behind the woman, stroking her shiny hair. After all the children in front had been served, the woman tugged the girl around, gave her a piece, then winked with a grin. The girl blinked in response, apparently unable to manage the one-eyed movement.

A tear slipped down Olivia's cheek. What a beautiful scene. Pure grace poured out of the woman and bathed the children. With one last comment and a pat on the head of the closest child, she dismissed them. They scampered away, squealing over their good fortunes.

From her delighted expression, the woman enjoyed the encounter as much as the little ones had. She tucked the bowl back into the cooler, flopped her hat on her head, and checked for customers.

A shiver ran down Olivia's spine as the woman made eye contact. Her huge brown eyes seemed to peer into Olivia's soul as if they recognized her. But they'd never met. Olivia was sure of it.

She couldn't help but smile and walk toward her as a flower's drawn to the sun.

"Hello there." The woman spoke with bright cheery tones. "I saw you following my babies. Would you like to try my honey candy too?"

The burn in Olivia's cheeks must have been apparent. She resisted the urge to put her hands up to hide them. "Are all those children yours?"

Laughter poured out of the woman's eyes and mouth. "No. Not biologically, anyway. They're precious, though. They stop by to brighten my day whenever I'm here selling my honey."

She stuck her hand out. "I'm Carissa Pappas. It's a pleasure to meet you."

Olivia accepted the proffered hand, letting the woman's brown eyes draw her in. So strange, yet so comfortable. "Olivia."

"I'm glad to meet you. May I offer you a candy? They're homemade, but the children love them."

Her cheeks burned once more. Being broke stunk. "Thanks. I'm good though."

Carissa pulled the bowl out anyway, lifted the lid, and held it out. "Oh, go ahead. It's on the house. I love giving out samples." She tipped her head to one side, her slinky black hair slipping over one shoulder. "It's good for business."

With a nod, Olivia selected one of the amber blobs and placed it on her tongue. It had been a long time since she'd experienced candy. She closed her eyes and did her best not to groan with pleasure.

When she opened her eyes again, Carissa grinned with a shared secret. "I know—wonderful stuff, huh?"

"Thank you." Olivia moved the candy to her cheek to slow its pace of dissolving. "It's been a while."

"You're very welcome. Are you working today?"

Nick. Absorbed in following the children, she'd forgotten. Rob better be with the woodpile, protecting it from theft.

All the same, she was grateful to have met this beautiful woman. One more question burned to be released before she was ready to return to her responsibilities, though.

"I'd love to learn about bees. Do you raise them yourself?"

Carissa cocked one eyebrow. "Really? Most people are afraid of getting stung. But yes, I do. I'd love to show you sometime."

Stung?

Olivia's breath hitched. Was the threat worth the sweet results? She'd already made a deal for chickens, which meant eggs. Bees would mean honey. But would that be enough? With the gardening results so poor, they hadn't any leftovers to can. Once winter hit, hunger would set in.

The negative vibes must have shown on her face because Carissa's warm, suntanned hand touched hers. "You okay?"

Why did she have to be an open book? "I'm good. Just thinking about the bees. I'd like to try it. How often do you get stung?"

"Here and there. Nothing worth doing is pain free. But hey… you're Wonder Woman, right? You can do anything you set your mind to."

Yeah right. If she only knew.

"Well, I need to get back to my woodpile. It was nice meeting you, Carissa."

"Lovely to make your acquaintance as well, Olivia. Don't be a stranger."

For some crazy reason, walking away from the person she'd just met felt wrong. That made no sense. What was Carissa's hold over her?

Enthralled in following the children, Olivia hadn't paid much attention to how she'd gotten to the honey table. The market area covered dozens of acres surrounding the auction barn. Though she thought she'd headed in the correct direction, she found herself by a wood line beyond the sales area.

This wasn't the way.

She skirted the area to find the way the children had come in. After about fifteen minutes, she neared the food pantry table their neighbors, the Worthingtons, manned. The sight caused her to pause.

Just months ago, her former friends would have welcomed her to the table. Jan Worthington, along with their neighbors Lizzy and Renee, used to invite her over to the farm to help in the gardens. Picking green beans knowing they'd end up in canning jars, ready to warm and eat, had been exciting.

The Worthington home sported solar panels on the roof, which provided enough electricity for fans, kitchen appliances, and hot showers. The thought of soaking in a warm tub made her go weak in the knees.

What would happen if she walked up to the table as if nothing had happened? Perhaps they wouldn't hold Rob's deception against her. They gave food away to people every time they set up at the market. Long lines led to that table. Surely, they wouldn't send her away if she asked.

Her stomach rumbled. Those canned beans in crates under the table… What she wouldn't give to have one of those jars, the beans so plump and salted. Forget warming them up. She'd eat them right out of the jar.

She started toward the table to join the queue and ask for whatever they'd be willing to share. Then she saw him.

Caleb Worthington. She recognized the lazy way his dark hair poked out around the rim of his baseball cap like he needed a haircut—all the time. He stood at the table, chatting with a customer. Her heart skipped a beat when his blue eyes peeked from under the rim.

That was it. She headed in the opposite direction.

Rob had ruined it. He'd betrayed Caleb's trust. They'd been best friends, and Rob allowed someone to use him to blackmail Caleb and his family, to steal what they had when they gave so much away.

She couldn't face him. She was guilty by association, and

Caleb had been right to ban Rob from returning to the farm.

Fifteen minutes later, she found the woodpile. But something was wrong. Half of it was gone. How could that be? They were supposed to deliver it to Nick.

Had Nick found another way to pick it up? Had Mr. Donahue come back early to load the truck?

She didn't see Rob. Danger signals sprinted up and down her spine. Picking up the pace, she jogged the rest of the way to find him.

When she got there, the bag of cracked corn slumped at the side of the half-full pile. Nick had been good at his word and brought the first part of the payment.

But where was Rob? And where was the rest of the wood? No sign of Mr. Donahue, so he hadn't taken the wood back to his truck.

She walked to the other side of the stack and groaned. Her cousin leaned against the woodpile with his jacket stuffed behind his head—snoring.

Well, didn't he look comfortable?

She shook his shoulder.

He mumbled something unintelligible but didn't wake. Within seconds, the snoring resumed.

A half-empty mason jar sat on the ground beside him, the clear liquid a familiar sight.

Jerk.

She'd sold the whole pile of wood while he spent the morning finding booze. Didn't take him long to indulge either.

"Rob." She got loud this time. He needed to tell her where the wood went. "Wake up. Where's the wood?"

He didn't even open his eyes, just grunted. "Stop."

A sick feeling swirled in the pit of her stomach. Had he given half the wood away for booze?

No. Not after she'd made a deal. She shoved his shoulder hard, knocking the jacket from behind his head. "I need to know where the rest of the wood went. Wake up."

He blurted out expletives as he rubbed the back of his head. "I sold it. Where'd you think it went?"

She saw red. "Didn't you see the Sold Out sign? I'd already *sold* the entire load."

Venomous words spewed from his mouth as he stumbled. "You're a stupid idiot. It's not like we don't have more back at the house."

No point in arguing with a drunk.

"Fine. I see my customer dropped off the chicken feed. He was supposed to give you the address to drop the wood at."

His face scrunched, his jaw slackening.

"Rob. What address did he give you?"

He flushed scarlet. "I don't remember. Stop pushing."

Her fists balled at her side as her internal temperature rose. So that was it. There was only a half load left, and no one to deliver it to.

Great. Just perfect.

Without enough time to sell the rest of the pile, it would go to Mr. Donahue, as per their agreement.

Hopefully, Nick would understand when she didn't show up with his order.

If not, she lost not only the sale but also potentially her best customer ever.

Well, no sense stewing in her frustration. She couldn't eat wood, so she grabbed an armload and headed out to see if she could make a last-minute trade. Anything edible would do.

4

Chapter Four

Sweat dripped from Olivia's face, and perspiration soaked her shirt sleeves. Her back ached after unloading the wood. They'd stacked it extra high today in the hope she'd find Nick to deliver his load and still have some to sell at the market for food.

Light-headed, she pressed stick fingers to her forehead. Too much work after too few calories at breakfast.

Aunt Amanda's pale face gleamed as well.

Ryan Donahue came from behind the mound, a sack of grain hefted high on his shoulder. "Where do you want the bag of chicken feed?"

She winced at the sight of the grain. When she'd brought it home, it rested in the corner of their kitchen. Rob and she argued over whether to dip into it. She'd planned to feed it to a flock of chickens to provide eggs for the family. Hens they hadn't been able to get as payment.

Rob voted to turn the cracked corn and wheat into gruel, and she'd been tempted to agree. But that would only solve a short-term problem, so she'd dragged it into her bedroom that evening. Best to keep it out of sight until they could bring it back to the market.

Olivia motioned toward two uncut rounds of wood they'd brought to sit on. "Could you set it behind our stools for us?"

Mr. Donahue heaved the sack off his shoulder onto the ground where she'd pointed. "Anything else I can do for you before I go?"

Aunt Amanda smiled at him as she sank onto the makeshift chair. "No thank you. We're all set."

"You don't look so good." He pulled off his work gloves, slapped them together to shake off sawdust, then jammed them in his coveralls pocket. One hand rubbed his jaw as he frowned at Aunt Amanda, then Olivia. "You two eat breakfast? Did you bring water?"

Olivia picked up her backpack from behind her stump and handed her aunt the thermos. "We're feeling the heat today. Pretty hot for fall. You'd never know we needed to double the blankets last night."

As Aunt Amanda drank, Mr. Donahue raised an eyebrow and crossed his arms. "Do you have lunch in that sack?"

If only.

"Planning to buy some."

Those soupy grits for breakfast hadn't been hearty enough for the tasks they'd accomplished so far. Besides the fact that Mr. Donahue only had room for two, Uncle Kevin had been there to load the truck, but he'd stayed behind to make sure Rob didn't burn the house down or come up with some other sort of alcohol-fueled lunacy.

Rob's father was the only one who could stand up to him when he was in drinking mode. He had to run out of booze soon, didn't he? He must be restocking somehow, which would explain his long disappearances from the house.

Mr. Donahue uncrossed his arms, shook his head, and huffed a deep breath. "Look, I'm already behind on my route. You two look like a puff of wind could blow you away. Get some food and make sure you stay hydrated."

Olivia's nod and smile seemed to appease him, and he headed to his truck. Mr. Donahue was right. Aunt Amanda's shirt hung off her bony shoulders, and her face was sallow. Hollowed cheeks made her smile come across as a grimace.

"Don't look at me that way." Aunt Amanda patted the wood stump beside her. "You don't look so hot yourself."

If Olivia looked anything like she felt, then it wasn't a pretty sight. Taking a seat would feel so good right now. Perhaps it would relieve the dizziness threatening to send her to her knees.

But they had to get this wood sold. They needed food for the week. The lack of steady income, coupled with Rob's sale of half the wood for liquor, overwhelmed her some days.

The fight between Uncle Kevin and Rob last evening had been the worst yet. Rob's onslaught of curses escalated into a fistfight. His deluge of alcohol consumption worked against his aim, so Uncle Kevin just suffered a bruised shoulder.

As always, Rob apologized the next day and vowed he'd never do it again. They all knew better. Until they could get him dried out, he couldn't control his world—alcohol did. All they could do was limit his access to drink as best they could. But it was a losing battle.

Focus, Olivia.

She didn't have time to deal with her problem cousin. She needed to get this wood sold. No way could Aunt Amanda manage the walk about the market looking for trades. That left Olivia to travel while her aunt tended to the woodpile.

She pulled a second thermos from her pack and handed it to her aunt. "I'll head out to look for buyers. Here's more water. If we're lucky, I'll bring food back before lunch."

She slung the backpack over her shoulder, pushed her arm through one strap, then poked her other arm through the second band. With only one thermos in the bag, it was light enough to carry for the day. If only the weather were cool enough to go without it. Even the water's slight weight felt like more than she could handle.

Knowing what to look for, she scanned the air above the market for telltale smoke. A few vendors stoked fires this morning, and she headed toward the closest one.

At the base of the fume, an elderly gentleman stirred a caldron with an oar-shaped paddle. Sweet-scented steam emanating from the pot told her all she needed to know about the contents.

A gray-haired woman manned the nearby table. They'd displayed jars of black sorghum molasses in single file. What she would give to have biscuits, much less the sticky syrup to slather on them.

Her mouth watered. She stepped up to the table and forced a chipper lilt into her voice. "Morning, Miss Annabelle. I see Mr. Charles is hard at work already. How are you doing with your wood stock? I've got some nicely dried logs today. It'll keep that fire hot until he's finished."

Miss Annabelle's toothy grin revealed a darkened incisor.

Olivia flinched. A dentist was hard to find these days.

"It's good to see you, dear." Miss Annabelle pushed a jar toward Olivia. "How much wood will this get me? Delivered, of course."

The sun's rays twinkled in the jar's diamond divots. "Two armloads sound about right?"

She'd hoped for two jars today. One to take home and one to negotiate for grits. Just the thought of being able to sweeten the morning bowl instead of the bland porridge made her stomach growl.

Miss Annabelle must have heard the rumble since she pushed a second jar to join the first. "Maybe a double load."

Olivia's cheeks ached with her wide smile. "Yes, ma'am. I'll bring four armloads right away."

Eager to complete the deal, she made her way back to their woodpile. When she arrived, a man chatted with her aunt. Her heart rate quickened—Nick was back.

Barely believing her good fortune, she joined the pair.

Her aunt's tense face relaxed when Olivia put her hand on her thin shoulder. "We were discussing Nick's order."

This wasn't the carefree man she'd bargained with last week. Agitation now hardened his face—just as she'd feared.

"Hello, Nick. I'm so sorry I missed you last time." She pointed to the feed sack behind the stool. "I brought back your feed since I couldn't deliver. But I'd love another chance."

He scowled and jerked his thumb toward Aunt Amanda. "I informed this lady I'd left my address when I dropped off the chicken food. Waiting a week for delivery wasn't the agreement."

Her aunt shuddered.

Time to smooth this out.

"Of course, that wasn't our deal." Olivia gave her aunt a calm squeeze and her customer her most apologetic smile. "My cousin wasn't feeling well that day. The address slipped his mind by the time I'd returned."

Nick huffed. "Not feeling well? I'd say something else got that boy's brain boondoggled."

Her face flushed. Even when he wasn't around, Rob's reputation hurt her business dealings. But maybe, just maybe, she could still close this sale. Perhaps if she let her cousin drop, Nick would focus on business.

"I'd love to get your wood delivered right away." She waved toward the enormous pile. "We've got your order right here."

She held her breath, waiting for his response.

He scowled at the ground, kicking his toe into the gravel. When he made eye contact, he grinned. "I can't say no to a pretty girl like you. After all, I've got hens at my house ready for pickup."

Her breath whooshed out, and her knees wobbled with her relief. Today's haul would be exceptional.

«»

They pulled up to a Victorian in the nearby town of Manchester. It was all Olivia could do to keep her jaw from dropping at the two-story redbrick behemoth. An enormous oak tree, dressed in lacy Spanish moss, shaded the front porch. A swing and wicker chairs offered a cozy place to view the property from. Dormer windows and turrets charmed her while the scent of a saltwater pool drifted from nearby. Most likely behind the house.

What would it be like to have the money to maintain a pool and live in a grand home such as this? Someone even mowed the lawn, so they either wasted precious fuel on a lawnmower or had a hand-push model. Who had time for that these days?

She opened her door. "I'll knock. He said he'd be home."

Aunt Amanda touched Olivia's arm. "Want me to go with you?"

"No, it's fine."

Mr. Donahue grumbled as he rolled his window down. "Hmm. Holler if you need me."

Olivia's boots clomped on the steps and porch before she used the huge knocker to announce her presence. Soft footsteps approached from the other side. The door cracked, and a petite girl flicked a glossy brown hair over her shoulder. "May I help you?"

"I'm here to deliver firewood. Nick is expecting me."

The young woman couldn't have been much older than Olivia—perhaps early twenties. Her frilly top showed generous cleavage while tight-fitting jeans revealed a thin frame. With a nod, she opened the door wider and waved her inside. "Wait here." The girl's sneakers squeaked as she pivoted and headed toward the back of the home.

Shiny wood floors gleamed beneath the sunlight spilling in, and the smell of polished wood banisters emanated from a staircase. A well-appointed living room beckoned from the door to her left, and a door on her right indicated another room. Light bathed the living room, casting a glow on quality furniture that matched Nick's rich lifestyle.

Heavier footfalls headed her way, and he sauntered around the corner at the end of the hallway.

"Good to see you kept your word." He stopped once he reached her. His hands went into the pockets of his pressed khakis, and his red polo was immaculate. "I confess, I wasn't sure you'd show."

She waved toward the truck. "Just point out your wood stash, and we'll offload."

Fortunately, the driveway led to the shed, so they didn't have to carry the wood far. Mr. Donahue backed the truck up to the building, and they unloaded and restacked the firewood.

Her stomach rumbled. Earlier, she'd been able to trade the second jar of molasses for five pounds of grits and a loaf of acorn bread. She'd shared half the loaf with her aunt and saved the rest for the men. The heavy food filled her belly, but this second round of hard work left her hungry for more.

Nick came through the fence surrounding the backyard pool and met them at the shed. He peeked inside and nodded. "Come on. I'll need some help to carry your new flock."

Mr. Donahue pulled the dog cage out of the truck bed, and they followed Nick through another fenced area into a garden with an enclosed chicken pen. A cat slunk past the coop and two wire cages with six hens in each.

He pointed to the enclosures. "As promised."

Aunt Amanda kneeled near the hens. "They're beautiful."

He smoothed his shirt and singled Olivia out. "I'd like to show you something if you have a minute while they load the birds."

What was that all about?

"Um, sure." She nodded to Mr. Donahue. "Can you help Aunt Amanda with the birds? I won't be long."

Mr. Donahue narrowed his eyes but gave a slow nod.

Nick swept his arm toward the fence gate. "Shall we?"

She scooted ahead of him and through the gate, then followed him to the house. Once there, he pointed across the street at another Victorian, like his, but painted bubble-gum pink.

"I own that home as well. I have rooms for rent—if you're interested." He hooked his thumb back toward the truck where Mr. Donahue and Aunt Amanda loaded the chickens. "Couldn't help but notice you live with your extended family.

Seems like you end up doing a lot of work for them. Ever think of striking out on your own?"

Her own place to escape Rob's drama seemed too much to ask for. No way could she afford such a thing since she had no way of earning a living. The wood they sold came from her family's woods. She owned no resources of her own.

But wouldn't it be grand? A girl could dream—couldn't she?

5

Chapter Five

Heaven. Olivia must have died and gone to heaven. Having a poached egg to accompany her morning grits was the best thing since sliced bread. Wait… sliced bread… that would be amazing too.

Sigh.

Perhaps someday.

She'd gotten up just as the sun was painting the sky pink. She couldn't sleep knowing she had chickens in the shed waiting to be let out to forage for the day. Who would have thought she'd find two eggs in the pine straw nest she'd created for them? *Two* of them. On top of that, the electric grid was up today, which meant she could cook the grits fresh and boil water for the eggs.

A hot protein-filled breakfast. Heaven.

The guilt of eating them both herself, before the others were even out of bed, tugged at her conscience. But the chickens were her idea. She'd researched how to raise them, spending as much time as she could afford to help chicken vendors set up and take down at the market. All so she could learn what they needed to keep the birds alive, healthy, and laying eggs.

Rob had scoffed. "We can't even keep bean plants alive, and you're going to try raising animals? Good luck!"

Uncle Kevin had been no more supportive. "But we don't have a chicken coop. If you don't keep them locked up, they'll run away."

At least her aunt had supported her, saying, "Olivia can figure it out. Give her a chance to try."

Besides, she had a dozen chickens. The bright tones of their legs, beaks, and wattles promised they were young enough to lay an egg a day. So, they might get ten more eggs today! Plenty to share.

She washed her plate as soon as she finished eating, scouring away the yellow evidence of her consumption. By the time Aunt Amanda trudged into the kitchen, Olivia had the dishes dried and put back in the cabinet.

Her aunt's eyes looked red and watery. Nothing like going through ragweed season with no allergy medication. "Good morning. You're up early."

Olivia pulled a chair out for her aunt, who might fall over if she didn't sit. After scooping grits into a bowl, she handed her aunt a spoon with the dish. "I couldn't wait to let the chickens out to hunt for bugs. The more protein they eat, the healthier those eggs will be."

"Thank you." After accepting the food, her aunt scooped a spoonful of molasses from the jar and stirred it into her porridge. "I sure hope you know what you're doing. We lost an entire load of wood to buy those birds. It's a risk."

Olivia's cheeks burned. Like any of them had some grand plan to get their food supply in better shape. If she left it up to them, they'd keep burning as many calories to collect and sell firewood as they brought in with the food they traded for. They'd all lost significant weight. How much longer did they think they could keep the routine up?

She clamped her lips together, tempted not to share any eggs. But, of course, she'd share—eventually. When the next batch arrived. Even now, her secret indulgence burned hot in her cheeks.

Sucking in a deep breath, she closed her eyes. She didn't need to be selfish. It wasn't their fault that they couldn't think ahead. Wrapped up in dealing with Rob, they couldn't see the bigger problem. They had to take in more calories than they spent. Losing weight the way they were wasn't safe. They needed to gain some.

She sat across from her aunt and cringed as her hand quivered to scoop grits from the bowl and bring them to her mouth. Her hollowed cheeks and bony fingers gave her a birdlike appearance.

Guilt dragged at Olivia's insides. "We'll have eggs for supper tonight, maybe even lunch today."

"That would be nice." With her aunt's response so devoid of life, it was almost as if she weren't talking to Olivia.

Uncle Kevin walked into the kitchen. "Let me guess—grits for breakfast. Am I right?"

As if they had any other food in the kitchen.

But his chipper voice suggested he was trying to start the day with a glass-half-full attitude. She stood and moved toward the stove. "Can I get you some?"

"I'd appreciate that."

As she got out a bowl and plopped grits into it, he gave her aunt a peck on the top of her head and sat beside her. After she handed him the warm bowl, he poured molasses into the concoction and dug his spoon in to stir. "You check on your chickens? It's your responsibility to keep them out of the garden. We don't need to lose any more food to them."

Don't do it.

It took every ounce of self-control not to roll her eyes. Here she was trying to bring protein into the house, and he was worried about cabbages. If it were up to her, she'd feed every plant to the birds and then enjoy the eggs. Talk about a straightforward decision. "Yes, sir. I'll go check the netting again."

What a relief to leave them in the dreary kitchen. Mornings were the quiet time of the day. Rob slept in, so there wasn't any arguing about him or with him.

Dew still clung to the tall grass around the house. Her jeans soaked in the moisture as she walked. No one had time to spare for mowing, and they didn't have a manual lawn mower, anyway. Gasoline wasn't something they could afford. Few people could these days.

The chickens hadn't wandered too far from their impromptu home. She'd been surprised when she first saw the flock. She'd expected all the birds to look the same, but she'd gotten a mixture of brown, black, and white. That made for a more interesting view.

She crossed her arms and leaned against the shed as they scratched in the lawn turned field, pecked at the ground, and ate blades of grass. There was a lot to learn about caring for them, but they were all plump and healthy looking—far healthier than their owners.

A quick count told her one was missing.

Oh boy. It better not have gotten carried off by a coyote already.

Squawking from the shed alerted her to the missing fowl's location. Her heart raced as she dashed into the shed, intent on finding a shovel to fight off whatever had attacked the bird.

When she rounded the corner, the hen lay in the pine straw nest, ruffling her feathers and squawking. Nothing appeared to be wrong, so why was she making so much noise?

Moments later, the hen half-jumped, half-flew off the nest, and in her place were two eggs—the cause of the ruckus.

"Ha! Look at you." Olivia chuckled at the bird sashaying away to join her sisters in the yard. "Good bird."

Were any eggs in the other nest? She edged closer. But the morning was still young, and they didn't all lay at the same time. Or so the farmer had told her.

The eggs warmed her palms as she scooped them up. Eager to show her prizes off, she jogged back to the house.

When she opened the door, she heard the last thing she wanted to. Rob was awake and had already triggered an argument.

"We don't need to cut wood every day."

She cringed at his surly voice as she walked through the doorway.

Her uncle stood glaring at his red-faced son. "Yes, we do. That's how we get the food on our table. We cut wood, and we sell it. It's called working for a living."

This old dispute. Somehow, Rob thought they only needed to cut wood the day before they went to market. His muddled faculties seemed to think they could cut an entire load in one day, even though they'd never pulled off such a feat.

Her news could cut through the tense situation, though. Once they saw what she had, they'd be too excited to fight. Walking over between Rob and his parents, she tried to draw their attention by holding out her hands, ready to display the treasure each held.

Just as she opened her palms for the big reveal, Rob swiped at her, growling. "Get your hands out of my face."

Her reactions weren't fast enough to hold on to the precious orbs, and both flew out of her hands, landing on the floor with loud cracks. Egg splattered the tile and their shoes, the golden yolks oozing out of the fractured shells.

She shuddered as she crouched to recover what she could. Then her anger flared hot. She glared up at her cousin. "Why? Why do you have to ruin everything?"

He spat out a curse, stomped on the broken egg closest to his sneakered foot, and stormed out of the room.

His last action turned the egg into a pulp of well-crushed shells and liquid. No way could she recover any of the mess now. The second one splatted in a smaller area. She tried to scoop up what she could. But the goo brought too much dirt from the floor with it.

Hot tears dripped from her cheeks, adding a salty mixture to the sticky mess on her hands.

Chairs clattered behind her. Then footsteps headed away from the table and down the hall toward Rob's room. An arm came around her shoulders, and her aunt kneeled beside her and whispered hot words against Olivia's hair. "I'm sorry. I hate that he ruined your surprise."

With those words, she lost the last of her control and let out the sobs she'd been trying to contain. It was too much. He was too much. No matter how hard she worked, he'd always spoil it.

It took a good while for her to get her feelings back in check and then clean up the mess. While she wiped the floor, her aunt filled thermoses with water for their day in the woods. Neither of them spoke. There was nothing to say.

Later, Olivia had more than enough time to ruminate as they toiled to saw, chop, stack, and then drag the firewood home. There wasn't much for her in her extended family's home. They were all slowly starving, despite their hard labor. The eggs would help, but seriously, would they be enough?

What if she took Nick up on the offer to get her own apartment? Perhaps that big house had enough room in the backyard to raise her own flock of chickens. Maybe she could also take Carissa's offer to learn about beekeeping.

If she did well enough, she could sell honey and eggs and find other jobs on the side. Perhaps she could even work with the other occupants to grow food. For all she knew, they already had a vegetable garden out there and ate spinach every night.

What would it be like to be independent? On her own two feet with no interference.

She worked side by side with her aunt to stack the wood beside the driveway. Uncle Kevin and Rob would be back from their last trip to the woods soon to add to the pile they'd collected for market day.

Her arms were the darkest tan she'd ever seen on them. Hours of outdoor labor gave them color and muscular definition but left them thin. She probably sported the fat level of an Olympian. But no gold medal glittered in her future.

Aunt Amanda dropped the last stick on the pile, then stretched her back like a cat after a long nap. The popping sounds emanating from her aunt's joints might have been funny if the circumstances were any different, but they both knew the work wore on her. She appeared much older than her forty-five years.

If only Olivia could relieve some of the workload or at least provide more nutrition to supplement. The chickens! "Want to come with me to check for eggs? We might have some for supper."

Her aunt gave a tired grimace. "I'm so tired. I need to sit. Do you mind checking without me?"

"Of course not."

They went in separate directions, her aunt to the house to get off her sore feet, and Olivia to the shed to see if the chickens had produced anything more.

The sight in the pine straw nests set her heart thumping in a joyful rhythm. Eight eggs of various sizes and shades waited for her trembling fingers to collect. Each of the twelve birds had produced today. Sure, she couldn't expect that every day, but seeing it on their first day made her want to skip. After carefully placing each of the orbs into a pouch she created with her shirtfront, she speed-walked to the house, then rushed into the living room where her aunt rested. "You won't believe it. Eight beautiful eggs."

Her aunt's expression at the sight of the treasure trove told the entire story. A tear slipped down her cheek as she stood to take in the view. With care, she took one egg in each hand, her eyes going as wide as the eggs.

"What a blessing." She wrapped Olivia into a gentle but firm hug, giving the egg nest in her shirt a wide berth. "I don't know what we'd do without you. Tonight, we feast!"

Olivia winced at a twinge of guilt. What made her think she could abandon her family? How would they make it if she left them alone to deal with Rob? He wasn't much help on the best of days. They didn't seem all that motivated to survive, much less thrive. Instead, the entire family lived in a deep depression.

When she studied her aunt, she saw a scarecrow—a shadow of a person. This was her family. Her blood. No way could she leave them. At least not right now. That apartment would have to wait.

6

Chapter Six

The bits of egg were a challenge to scrub off the skillet that evening, but Olivia didn't mind. She couldn't stop thinking about the egg scramble they'd enjoyed for supper. Chopped chives she'd found in the front yard gave them a zippy flavor—she wanted more. Eight eggs didn't go far when you were so protein starved.

The worst of it might be behind them, though, now that eggs were on the menu. What a monumental accomplishment. She'd thought she'd feel satisfied with their lot once she wrangled the flock of hens. But now she wanted more. A satisfied stomach permitted her to dream. What would a normal life look like once they no longer had to think about survival?

Eggs were just the beginning of the solution for proper nutrition. Time for a new project.

Her time working on the Worthington farm proved there were plenty of options to bring variety to their table. If only she could connect with Jan again for more lessons. Perhaps she'd brave a solo mission to strike up a friendship with their neighbors again.

But was it safe to visit them? Not that long ago, they'd booby-trapped the driveway leading to their farm. They had to protect themselves from marauders and had done so just in time to avoid losing their farm. What if those traps were back in place?

She'd heard how they put out warning signs to protect the innocent when they expected an attack. But what if they'd set trip wires without warnings this time? Visiting uninvited could be dangerous. Better to make a special trip to find their table at the market this week. See if Jan and her family would have her out to call on them again.

She made her way outside once she slid the last pan in the cabinet. Her aunt and uncle rested on the porch swing. "Dishes are done."

A lawn chair that had seen better days waited opposite the swing, and she claimed the seat.

Aunt Amanda looked less pale tonight. Or was it Olivia's imagination? "Thank you, dear. Supper was amazing. I'll confess I doubted your idea of getting chickens, but I can say I was mistaken."

Uncle Kevin nodded. "You were right. I was wrong. I didn't realize we wouldn't have to feed the chickens right away."

Finally. They saw the light.

"We'll have to feed them during the winter—once there aren't as many bugs and plants to eat. But for now, it's just making sure they have a source of water."

She crossed her legs at the ankles and leaned back in the chair. Bats flew overhead, collecting bugs in their flight paths. Fireflies glowed in the weeds and on the trees.

The hens all filed into the shed at sundown, and she closed the door behind them. As long as they were safe at night when the predators were most active, they should be fine during the day.

The birds had plenty of places to hide if a hawk targeted the flock. A rooster would help protect them, but she needed to learn to candle before she brought a male in. Using a light source was the only way to tell if a rooster had fertilized an egg, but she hadn't learned the specifics yet. The last thing she wanted was to crack one open, only to find a baby chick. One farmer shared how he'd found one half grown in an egg he'd forgotten to check, then cracked into a pan.

Yuck.

That was a problem for another day. Right now, she was just going to savor her victory… and plot her next step. She couldn't let it go. It was like solving a giant jigsaw puzzle. Only the reward was survival. Who knew, if she played this game right, they might even thrive.

«»

Uncle Kevin dropped the ax at the foot of the woodpile. "I'm going to see if I can get the tools sharpened today. So, I'll need you to mind the store while I search for someone with a honing steel."

Mr. Donahue hadn't yet arrived to transport them and the wood to the market, and she grew impatient. Her uncle's plan didn't fit with her own. "But I was going to see if I could trade for some molasses today. We're almost out."

He frowned. "Well, you're going to have to hope I find what I need first. If we don't get these tools sharpened, we aren't going to have much wood to sell next week. Then what?"

He was right. But she'd also wanted to check on the price of rabbits and cages and a few other things, including a talk with Jan. But no reason to go into every detail of her strategy for the day. After all, she was always the one who did the walkabout. She was their best negotiator, and they all knew it.

Rob only bargained for booze or items that benefited him. Her aunt wouldn't stand up to any bully who wanted to negotiate her down until she was almost giving things away. Uncle Kevin got into a fight at least once per day, as he got too competitive for the best deal.

Mr. Donahue's hybrid truck pulled into the driveway in stealth mode. At least, that's how she thought of it when it was running on the quiet electric battery. Once the wood filled the bed, it would require the gas-powered engine to deliver them and the load to market.

"Morning, folks." He stepped out of his truck and hooked his thumbs by his coveralls bib. "I see it's the usual today. Let's get loaded up. Should be a beautiful day."

Uncle Kevin bellowed. "Amanda! Rob!"

Her aunt opened the door and came out to help—no sign of Rob.

"Where is that kid?" Her uncle grumbled as he walked toward the house. "I swear I'm going to tan his hide if he doesn't get his rear end out here."

Halfway between the truck and the house, her aunt and uncle met, and she spoke to him in subdued tones. He threw his hands up in the air and stomped back to the truck.

He growled at Olivia and Mr. Donahue. "Let's get it done."

Great. Rob was in a mood, and rather than make him help, they'd do his part of the work. She was so sick of it.

Frustration's slow burn was still hot in her brain when they arrived at the market and unloaded the firewood. The ride had been a silent one, even though Mr. Donahue had tried to drum up a conversation.

Drama seemed to dominate her life. At least wherever Rob was involved.

Before he walked away, Olivia tried to negotiate one more time with her uncle. "I really would like to do some shopping before we leave if I can."

He sighed, then nodded. "I'll do my best."

By the time the sun was at high noon, she'd bargained about a quarter of the woodpile away for jars of green beans, pinto beans, and four pounds of ground corn. Now that she had eggs, if she could get more molasses, she could make cornmeal biscuits. Wouldn't that be a treat? Her mouth watered. It had been too long since she'd had one fresh out of the oven.

A gaggle of children frolicked past her. Most likely the same group that visited Carissa with the tiny girl tailing them. As they passed by, Olivia smiled and remembered their trip to the honey table. That was probably their current destination. Too bad she couldn't follow them and bask in the older woman's smile.

What about that woman was so appealing? She was like sunshine on two feet. You couldn't be around her and not feel like smiling.

Olivia needed to smile today.

A breeze came through and carried the scent of molasses, tempting her to abandon her post for a quick walk around the vicinity.

Risky. Not everyone could afford to be honest these days. Better not.

"Hey, there. How goes it?" Jan Worthington grinned at her, hands on hips and gun strapped to her belt.

No words would come.

"Oh, come here, silly." Jan pulled Olivia into a hug. "We're still friends, aren't we?"

Were they? She'd love to believe so.

After Jan released her, Olivia shoved her hands into her back pockets. "Sure. I guess so."

Her former friend looked fantastic. Shiny hair, sparkling eyes, and rosy cheeks showed the farm was doing well.

Jan's eyes narrowed as they roamed Olivia's face and body. "You're skin and bones. Don't they feed you?"

A laugh erupted before she could contain it. "We make do, though we don't have the gardening talents you do."

Hands back on her hips, Jan's mouth twisted. "Why haven't you been to the food pantry table? We're here every week. It's not that long of a walk to the other side, you know."

Olivia shrugged. Surely Jan knew her brother told Rob he was no longer welcome on their farm. Or at least that was Rob's version. Pulling off her ball cap, Olivia fingered through her own sweat-tangled dry hair, feigning indifference. "We're pretty busy over here. Lots of wood to sell."

Liar! She'd avoided the end of the market where they stationed the food pantry.

Jan raised an eyebrow. "Who's here helping you today? Rob?"

Like he was any help.

"No, Uncle Kevin is out looking for sharpening services. I'll tell him you stopped by."

The other eyebrow went up. "You trying to get rid of me?"

Rats. This wasn't going well at all.

If her spine stiffened any more, she'd be a statue. "No, of course not."

"So, what can I bring you from the food pantry?" Jan's toe nudged the cans by Olivia's feet. "I see you've got a few staples there. What are you low on?"

Where to begin?

"We're good. Thanks, though."

She didn't want handouts. She wanted to learn to run a flourishing farm. Why couldn't she find the words to say that?

Jan waved a hand in exasperation and slapped it back down on her thigh. "Really? Are we going to play a game here? If you don't tell me what you want, I'll bring back what I think you might need. Then what good will that do? You might end up with ten jars of green beans, then how would you feel?"

Ten jars of green beans? That wasn't a threat. If only it was a promise.

"No, honest. I'm going to do more shopping after Uncle Kevin gets back. We're good."

Jan's responding glare spoke volumes.

Perhaps this was a good time to change the subject.

Olivia dug her boot into the dirt and kicked a stone her toe unearthed. "I need one favor if you wouldn't mind."

"What's that?"

"Could I come to the farm so you could teach me about raising rabbits? I know your folks got some last year. I'd love to learn how."

Last year, a young boy, Jacob, and his mother joined the Worthingtons on their farm. Jacob had pestered Jan and her father until they allowed him to get bunnies. But Mr. Worthington had been adamant that they were for food and not pets.

Jan's face had broken out into a huge grin, and her fist-pumping cheer just lacked a pom-pom. "Not only *can* Jacob show you, but he'd also love to. I'm sure he'll give you a doe. You'd just need to go find a buck from another vendor to mate."

Olivia's face burned. "I'm not looking for a handout."

Jan spun and walked away. "Didn't think you were."

Uncle Kevin returned not long afterward, his ax and two saws freshly sharpened. She'd have just enough time to trade for molasses and a bit of acorn flour before they met up with Mr. Donahue for the ride home.

She was pleased with what she'd accomplished, even though Mr. Donahue's transportation fee for the day was almost a quarter of the truckload. She couldn't wait to get home and make cornbread biscuits.

At home, she laid her prizes on the table and went to set the oven to preheat. But the oven wouldn't turn on. Then it registered that there was no electricity in the house tonight. No oven. No baking tonight. *Rats.*

She closed the shed door after gathering the eggs while the hens settled on their roosts. She couldn't help but smile as she spoke to the birds. "You're going to get company, ladies."

Though her cousin and aunt had been home all day, neither had bothered to make a fire outside, so they ate cold green beans with leftover grits for supper. Quite the depressing meal after anticipating cornbread. They ate in silence, each stealing intermittent glances at the eggs in the wire basket waiting to be cooked.

She stacked green beans on her fork. Maybe she'd better, well, spill the beans. "I'm going to see Jan this weekend. She's going to teach me about rabbits."

Rob's head shot up from his sullen posture. Something dark flashed in his eyes. "We aren't allowed on that farm, remember? Why would you even want to go there? Find some other place to learn."

That was it. Her fork clattered to her plate. She was tired of him bossing her around.

"No." She stiffened her spine. "Jan's my friend. I don't care what you think of them. She invited me, and I'll go."

He slammed the table with his palms as he stood, then strode out of the kitchen and down the hallway. The crack of his bedroom door against the frame finished his tantrum.

"Robert!" Her aunt chided as her uncle stood looking imposing.

As if it mattered when Rob wasn't even there to see it.

Shaking, Olivia left the table to go to her room. At least she made it behind her privacy door before she broke into sobs.

How much more of her cousin's surly attitude could she take? All she wanted was for them to be fed—though it would be nice if someone cared how she felt once in a while. If it hadn't been for Rob's stupid maneuver to blackmail Caleb, they'd all still be friends. She'd be part of building up the food pantry instead of a potential recipient. Being friends with the Worthington crew was worth everything now. But it was all gone—because of her drunk of a cousin.

Exhaustion pulled her into sleep after she'd cried herself dry.

Her eyes sprang open to darkness. No moon to light her room tonight. She wasn't sure what woke her, but the hairs on her neck rose to attention.

As she lifted herself, a hand clamped over her mouth and pushed her back down into her pillow. A boozy breath tickled her ear, and a hoarse whisper accompanied the sharp pinch of a blade against her neck. Rob's voice grumbled next to her ear. "You go to that farm, I'll kill you. I mean it. I'll... kill... you."

Chapter Seven

The thundering in Olivia's ears wouldn't clear. She heard Rob's whispered threats, but couldn't comprehend what he said. Frozen in place, she didn't dare move. If only she could shrink into nothing—disappear into the sheets.

Perhaps if she didn't react, he'd give up and leave. Tears slid down the sides of her face, pooling in her ears.

It felt as if he'd never stop. His vaporous breath was moist in her ear. The hand not holding the knife pushed into her. A trickle slid down her neck near the blade. Blood? Sweat? Tears?

If only her aunt or uncle would hear him and rescue her. But his lowered voice was barely audible inches from her face.

He swore under his breath—cursed her. The next sentence she understood. "You will not go to that farm, will you?"

What could she do? If she moved, the knife might dig into her flesh.

Her silence wasn't what he wanted. "Answer me."

Though her mouth opened and breath exited her lips, no

sound would come out. Her throat was tight—too narrow for words to escape.

She forced herself to pull a lungful of air in through her nose and tried once more.

A single word emerged in a breathy whisper. "No."

"That's right. You won't, because if you do, you're dead." Then with one more expletive, he slid away from her, the knife gliding from her neck.

Not daring to move, she waited in the dark for any signs he was still in the room. After a few minutes with no sounds, she allowed herself to sob, quietly at first. Then she buried her face in the pillow and gasped cries.

How did her life get to this point? Nothing had been right since the collapse—since Mom died. It had been bad enough when her father started drinking. But when they had to live on the streets, never able to sleep in peace, she'd thought that was the lowest her life could get.

A bitter laugh bubbled up. She no longer needed to worry about strangers threatening to kill her in her sleep—her own family took care of that now.

Thoughts swirled in her head as she drifted into a light sleep, waking at every creak or groan of the house.

When the sun's rays pinked the horizon, it was time for action.

With the dawn of the new day came clarity. This house was no longer safe. Rob had never been the friendliest person. But since he'd started drinking, a darkness in his eyes grew by the day. Though the egg debacle hadn't been the first time he'd taken a swipe at her, she'd never imagined he'd pull a weapon.

Now, he'd taken his alcoholism to the next level. So she needed to take her survival plan up a notch.

With as much speed and silence as she could muster, she stuffed her clothes and personal items into a pillowcase. Fear made her clumsy. Her frantic fingers struggled to tie knots in the fabric to safeguard its contents.

She lugged her backpack out of the closet and added the last items into it. Then she surveyed her room for what she'd miss if she left it behind. The cheap wooden frame on her dresser cradled the only picture she owned of her onetime family.

Mom and Dad stood behind her with the iconic Disney castle in the background. Her mother wore the same silly ears as her twelve-year-old self. Dad had refused to don anything he considered undignified. It hadn't mattered to her, though. Back then, she was still his princess.

She tucked the frame into the backpack's front pouch, secured the zipper, and tied her clothing-filled pillowcase to the backpack.

The door made no sound when she opened it and slipped into the hallway. As she tiptoed toward the kitchen, her heart leaped into her throat when she heard Rob's voice. She froze.

Behind his bedroom door, he mumbled, "No. I didn't mean it."

She peeked in through the crack. Then sagged against the wall, letting out a held breath. He was in bed… dreaming. He thrashed in his sleep. Must be a nightmare—better in his sleep than hers. She continued past his room.

She didn't stop once she reached the kitchen. Instead, she eased the front door open and deposited her bag on the porch before sprinting to the shed. When she let the chickens out, she crossed to the two nesting boxes and gathered five eggs. "Good birds."

She cradled the fragile eggs. What were the chances she

could keep them whole as she fled? They'd be useless to her broken. Could she risk the time to boil them? She ran a fingernail over the brownish shells. One already had a crack.

Wasting no time, she ran back to the house and said a silent prayer there would be electricity this morning. In front of the stove, she could barely contain her happy dance as the clock on the stove flashed that it needed to be reset.

"Thank you, God."

Getting a pan out of the cabinet and filling it with water in silent mode was no easy feat, but she managed it. The family rarely got up early. Long days filled with manual labor gave them all the incentive to retire early and sleep in late. Still, she wanted to be out of the house before they rose. She couldn't face any of them right now.

They say a watched pot never boils. Though it seemed an eternity, hers eventually did, with all five eggs resting at the bottom of the water-filled pan. She stared at the blinking clock so she could time the eggs. Exactly thirteen minutes. That's how long her mom taught her to cook a hard-boiled egg.

While she waited, she pulled two thermoses out of the cabinet and filled them with water. She deposited both in the backpack on the front porch before she returned to the kitchen to check the progression of time.

A bedroom door opening caused her heart to skip a beat. Should she make a dash for the front door? The breath she'd been holding released at the thud of the bathroom door closing. She checked the stove clock. Two more minutes. Surely, she could have just two more. While she waited, she pulled a plastic bowl and lid out of the cabinet and a dish towel from a drawer.

Should she take the eggs now—even though they'd still be runny? The last thing she needed was for her family to catch her in the kitchen before she could escape.

Escape. The word poked at her brain like a thorn stuck in her skin—an irritation pulling her focus away from reality. She stared around the room, taking in every inch of what had once been a well-appointed, functioning space. It had been a haven—until it wasn't. Perhaps it hadn't been safe for a while now, but she'd ignored it until Rob forced the issue. Probably. She let things go on for too long, ignoring the signs to her own peril. But she'd miss what she'd worked so hard to build.

No sound came from the hallway, but she didn't waste a moment past the thirteen-minute mark. She used a slotted spoon to scoop the eggs out of the pan. Then she dropped the eggs into the nest she'd made in the bowl with the dish towel, closing them in their cocoon.

She left the pot for her aunt to wash, turned off the stove, and hurried to the porch. After she stuffed the bowl in her backpack, she hefted the load onto her shoulders. How could such a meager assortment of personal possessions weigh it down so? But not nearly as much as a load of wood, and she'd carried that plenty of times.

It would be a few miles' walk into town if she took the highway, but it wasn't safe for a young woman to walk the roads alone anymore. Instead, she walked along a path within the woods where the brush was thinner.

Whenever she came to a home, she skirted it or crossed the road to the other side. Dogs barked and carried on as she passed too close for comfort. None of them were loose, and she made it safely to the outskirts of Manchester.

Once in the town, she took to the sidewalk, keeping her shoulders up high so as not to look like a victim. Dad taught her that years ago. Never look like the easy target. Let them pick someone else who looked weak.

Her feet ached by the time the candy-pink house came into view. Smoke drifted from the chimney of Nick's brick home across the street. His offer better still stand. She needed a place to stay, to call home, to find sanctuary.

The knocker on his wooden front door screamed for oil. When she lifted it, it didn't fall back down. Instead, she had to force it down once… twice… three times. Then she waited.

The same petite woman who'd answered the door the last time opened it for her. Her long brunette hair pulled away from her face into a ponytail. "Yes? May I help you?"

"I'm here to see Nick. He offered me an apartment." Olivia kept her hands at her sides, fighting the desperate urge to fidget, but stood still, trying to look confident.

The woman's eyes went wide, and she checked behind her. Then she came out onto the front porch, shut the door behind her, and lowered her voice to a whisper. "Find another apartment. This one's full."

No. She couldn't have lost her opportunity already. "But it was just days ago. Nick said there were rooms available."

The woman pushed her toward the stairs leading back to the sidewalk. "Find another place. Please."

How strange. The woman's eyes were pleading. Was this woman wanting the apartment for herself? Or for a friend? Or was there truly not another apartment available?

Nick's voice came from inside the house. "Nadine? Where'd you go? Is someone here?"

The woman jumped, glancing behind herself before hissing, "Please. Go."

No way was Olivia leaving until she'd confirmed with Nick. She crossed her arms over her chest and squared her shoulders.

"No, ma'am. I want to talk to Nick."

The door opened behind them, and Nick appeared. Blond hair darker when wet, he stood there buttoning the cuffs of his dress shirt. "I thought I'd heard a knock. Nadine, why didn't you invite our guest in? It's such a delight to see you again, Ms. Olivia."

Nadine scurried past Nick into the house, and Olivia followed her, happy to get her chance to speak to the owner. "I was hoping to talk to you about renting that apartment."

His thin lips spread out, sending a slight ripple through his short-trimmed beard. "What a pleasant surprise. I'd been hoping you'd be back. Of course, I've got just the perfect room for you. You'll love it."

Her legs wobbled. She'd been so worried Nadine was right and there wouldn't be a room. She had no desire to sleep on the streets again. Now came the tricky part.

"I'm afraid I don't have any cash right now. But I've got some opportunities lined up. I was hoping I could do some work around the house or the apartment to help cover my rent." Before he could object, she added, "Just for a little while, of course. It won't take me long to get a job. I'm a hard worker."

She couldn't quite interpret his lazy smile. Was he going to reject her offhand? What else could she offer?

"I'm sure we can work something out." His next words came like an answered prayer. He draped an arm around her. "Let's get you that room."

She felt a little conspicuous as the older man walked her across the street and rapped twice on the pink house's front door. A girl who couldn't be older than fifteen answered his knock, her blond hair pulled up into a butterfly bun atop her head. With the sparkly fairy on her T-shirt, she looked like a child. "Oh. Hey, Nick."

The girl ushered them both into the front parlor.

"Olivia, this is Emlyn. She lives here in one of the rooms as well. Emlyn, please escort Ms. Olivia to the vacant room on the third floor and make her feel welcome. She's looking for a new home, and we need to make sure she has everything she needs."

He cocked his head at Olivia then. "I've got appointments today, but I'll check in with you later to assure you've settled in. We can discuss the rent later."

After a slight bow, he left as quickly as he'd brought her in.

Her chest constricted, and her throat closed as she swallowed down a foreign awe. Could this be her home?

"Come on." Emlyn let out a giggle before flitting toward the staircase, fingers twitching in a beckoning wave as if spreading pixie dust. "You'll have a hike up to the third floor, but there are only two bedrooms up there. I just moved into the other one last week. So, we'll be neighbors."

The girl practically pranced up the stairs while Olivia trailed her. She didn't see anyone else as they ascended. "How many other people live here?"

Her guide walked sideways to make conversation as they continued to progress. "You're number eight. I'll introduce you to everyone at dinner."

Dinner. She'd not eaten yet today, and it had to be closing in on noon by now. Good thing she had eggs in reserve if she got hungry. "Does everyone eat together?"

"Yes, we take turns cooking and cleaning. Your name will get added to the schedule. But you get the first week off to get acquainted. I just started my turn helping last night."

Emlyn rapped on a door once as they went by. "My room."

She stopped in front of a second entry on the same wall. "Your new home."

She walked into the room, gesturing for Olivia to follow her. The space was small, but sunshine streamed through the window onto a twin bed with a pink comforter and frilly, laced pillow.

Olivia reached to touch the white dresser—her dresser now? The narrow closet stood open, showing a tiny area with one empty wire hanger.

Though it was only a single room in a house, it might still be well beyond her ability to pay. "How much do you pay in rent?"

"Don't know." Emlyn gave her a confusing shrug. "Nick said not to worry about it at first. He's a sweet guy."

Olivia slid the heavy pack off her back, and it bounced as it landed on the bed. "How so?"

Emlyn avoided eye contact and walked back to the door. "I got kicked out of my house. Mom's boyfriend moved in, and she accused me of flirting with him. Like that would ever happen." Her face scrunched up. "She said I had to go. I don't know what I'd have done if Nick hadn't found me and offered me a place to stay."

How could any mother do that to her daughter? Mom would never have done something like that. Nick must be the nicest guy Olivia ever met. She'd do whatever it took to fit in here. No matter what, she'd work her butt off to make the rent.

Whatever it took. She was home.

8

Chapter Eight

Emlyn left Olivia to unpack, so she sat on the bed to untie her pillowcase. As she pulled out the clothing she'd jammed into the impromptu luggage, the realization of what she'd done settled in.

She was on her own now. Alone.

Wrapping her arms across her chest, she closed her eyes. What had she done?

By now, her aunt and uncle would be up, wondering where she was. Perhaps she should have left a note. But what could she have said? *I'm sorry, but your son is a drunk and a homicidal maniac.*

Would they even know how to take care of the chickens? And what was she supposed to do here? She had nothing to sell or trade for more birds. Perhaps they already had birds and a garden—then what? If she had nothing to contribute to their efforts, she couldn't pay the rent. She'd be homeless.

For that matter, she didn't even know how much the rent was. How could she have been so stupid as to move in without even knowing what it would cost?

Maybe she should tell Nick she'd changed her mind and go back. If she told Aunt Amanda what Rob had done, she might protect her only niece-in-law.

Who was she kidding? They didn't even protect themselves.

Her lungs tightened, and she felt woozy. She hugged her legs to her chest, lowered her head between her knees, and wrapped her arms around her legs.

Deep breaths, kiddo. No need to panic yet.

For all she knew, Nick was good for his word and would help her like he'd helped these other girls. And she wasn't an imbecile. After all, who came up with the idea of getting chickens and worked out the deal? Which of her family was the best at negotiating in the market?

You, that's who!

A quiet tap at the door thrust her back to reality. "Yes?"

"It's me again, Emlyn. Lunch in a half hour. I can show you the rest of the place after lunch if you aren't ready yet."

"I'll be down in a minute."

Olivia removed her head from between her knees and sprawled back on the bed. After a dozen slow, deep breaths, she felt calmer. She stood and stretched her back, legs, arms, then finally her neck. Time to get a move on. Until she found a job, searching for one was her priority.

After she'd placed the last of her belongings in or on her dresser, she tossed her backpack into the closet. Taking her eggs and one of the water-filled thermoses with her, she set off to find the kitchen.

Emlyn was waiting for her at the second-floor landing, leaning against the dark-wood wainscot and stroking a calico cat in her arms. "There you are. Want that tour now?"

The animal eyed her suspiciously and jumped out of Emlyn's

arms and sauntered along the well-worn carpeted runner when Olivia tried to pet it. "I take it the cat isn't friendly."

With a quick brush of her clothing, Emlyn gave her a toothy grin. "That's Sam. She's an older cat and can be cantankerous. Doesn't like strangers, but she'll get used to you fast enough now that you're living here." She pointed at the bowl Olivia carried. "Whatcha got there?"

She held the bowl out to the other girl. "Hard-boiled eggs. I can contribute them to a meal. Meant to eat them for breakfast, but didn't get around to it."

Emlyn nodded and accepted the offering. "We love eggs. Nick raises chickens at the main house, and Nadine brings us extras that don't get sold on market day."

That had been Olivia's plan as well—to raise enough chickens to have eggs to spare and sell them. It had been an excellent strategy. If only her family had been supportive.

Oil lamps lit their descent down the stairs as Emlyn began her tour discussion. "So, the third floor is just you and me. The other girls share rooms on the second floor, two in each of the three larger bedrooms. Whatever you do, don't go into Stella and Molly's bedroom without asking. Stella will rip your head off." They passed the foyer and entered the dining room. "Obviously, this is the dining room, and the kitchen is right through here."

After dropping the bowl of eggs on the wood-topped kitchen island, Emlyn led the way through a narrow hallway that ended in an office. They exited the back door onto a patio overlooking a fenced yard. A pin oak tree hung half into the neighbor's yard and overshadowed one corner of the fence. An overgrown flowerbed sprawled out of its confines in the opposite corner, displaying equal quantities of intentional plantings and weeds.

The grass waving in the breeze reached her knees and had already gone to seed. No gardeners on this side of the road. Perhaps Nick might pay her to do the job. But she hadn't seen any of the other inhabitants on the tour, and no one was cooking either.

She reached to touch Emlyn's arm, then thought better of it, and dropped her hand. "Where is everyone?"

Emlyn shrugged. "Molly and Stella both had dates last night. They don't come home on date nights until the next afternoon. The other girls went to Nick's this morning. They had a job over there."

Hadn't come home from dates? And that was normal? Her mother would have skinned her alive if she hadn't come home at night. She could almost hear her now. "These girls have loose morals. You shouldn't be hanging out with them."

She could imagine Mom's horror over how the world changed after she died. How her daughter's world had changed. "I take it the older girls have steady boyfriends. Are they… engaged?"

"They don't talk about their personal lives. Once you get to know Stella, you'll see it's best to avoid subjects she avoids."

Great. She was living with girls who not only sleep around but were cranky to boot. But, like Dad always said, beggars can't be choosers, and she was grateful to have a place to land for now. Maybe Nick had other apartments she could rent once she started making money.

Speaking of which, she needed to nail down that job. Perhaps Emlyn had some ideas. "So, what do you do for work?"

Emlyn stuck her hands in the back pockets of her blue jean shorts and, barefoot, kicked her toe in the grass. "Nothing yet.

I never had a job before, except doing chores around the house. Nadine works in Nick's house, so not too likely I'll be able to get a job there. But I was hoping he had some rich friends who might need help."

Wealthy people weren't easy to find. Before things fell apart, most had their savings tied up in stocks, bonds, and businesses. The majority of which became worthless when the supply chains crumbled. These days, affluent individuals owned farms and had the resources to grow food. Like the Worthingtons.

Maybe she should have gone to their house first, instead of coming here. But their house was beyond full with the number of folks they'd taken in lately. The last thing they needed was one more mouth to feed. On top of that, what if Caleb didn't want her there? She wouldn't blame him after Rob's treachery. No, heading to their farm was too much of a risk.

She needed to rely on Nick's charity for now, but it wouldn't last long. There had to be other ways to earn a living.

They went back into the house to the kitchen. Two other girls were there. One with long, shiny, jet-black hair sat on a stool at the island. A book hid her face. The other girl's shoulder-length brunette hair framed her heart-shaped face. She stood on the opposite side of the island, slicing the boiled eggs over top of lettuce leaves. A cucumber lay on the counter.

Emlyn patted the brunette's arm in passing. "This is Brandy." She scooted over to the seated girl and nudged her book down. "And hiding behind this is Anna. Ladies, I'd like to introduce our newest housemate, Olivia."

Brandy's smile extended to her hazel eyes as she waved with the paring knife still in hand. "Welcome to the nuthouse." She twitched her head toward Anna, who'd ducked back into her book. "And this one's the nuttiest of them all."

Emlyn giggled, but Anna still didn't respond.

Brandy continued. "See what I mean? You've got to make an appointment with that one if you want to have a conversation."

The book slammed shut, revealing a flash of green eyes that squinted in a glare. Anna practically spat words at Brandy. "Just because the rest of you can't appreciate the art of the written word, doesn't mean you should interrupt without regard to where a person is at in a sentence."

Brandy stuck her tongue out at Anna, who returned the gesture.

Emlyn sighed. "Don't mind these two. They may fight like cats and dogs, but they're roommates and get along quite well when no one is looking."

Anna blinked up at Olivia, giving her a bright smile. "It's a pleasure to meet you, Olivia. Welcome to the pink house."

So that was what they called home. Kind of catchy. But… "I'm still trying to figure out how I'm going to pay rent here. What do you guys do for work? Maybe I can get a job wherever you're working?"

Brandy spoke first. "We haven't been here long. All of us, except for Molly and Stella, are new to the place. I ran away from home and was living in an old abandoned house when Nick caught me stealing at the market."

Her face pinked. "He was super nice about it, though. Said he didn't want me to get in trouble and asked why I was stealing. When I told him I was homeless, he offered for me to come here. He said it was like a mission for him—helping girls who were alone. I only began helping with chores this week."

That was weird. Everyone was new at the house except for the two oldest? Perhaps Nick had just started on his mission, as he called it. And why had Brandy run away from home? That hadn't been a safe move for a teenager before the world fell apart. Now it was downright insane unless her home was just as unsafe as Olivia's had been. Perhaps Brandy would share her story someday.

Brandy finished with the egg slicing, then started on the cucumber. "Just remember, I made lunch. Anna is in charge of supper."

The flash was back in Anna's eyes. "Everyone knows I'm in charge of supper. You don't need to remind me all the time."

Emlyn elbowed Olivia as if to emphasize the continued argument. "They can't stop. It'll last all day unless someone steps in."

Brandy ignored Emlyn and shot back at Anna. "I wouldn't have to remind you if you didn't always get lost in your books and forget your chores."

Jumping off her stool, Anna jammed a hand on her hip. "If you knew how to read, you'd be enjoying the library in this house too. It has all the classics and then some."

Brandy winced.

Anna sucked in a breath, then pulled her lips into her mouth as if she were trying to draw the words she'd said back out of the air. "I'm sorry. I didn't mean that."

No one said anything for a beat.

Then Emlyn broke the silence. "That salad looks amazing. Let's eat."

After lunch, Brandy worked on the dishes, and Anna offered to show Olivia the library. Once the two were alone, Anna whispered, "Brandy can read, but she has dyslexia. So it's hard for her, and she hates it. I shouldn't have said what I did."

"You seem close, almost like sisters. Have you been together long?"

"Not really, just since we moved into the apartments here, but we hit it off right away, almost like we'd known each other all our lives."

They climbed the stairs to the second floor, then headed left down the hallway past two closed doors. At the end of the hall, they entered the round room inside the house's turret. The windows allowed in plenty of light but had shades available to pull down to keep the direct sunlight at bay. Books filled the two floor-to-ceiling shelves lining each side of the door. Cozy overstuffed chairs crowded the room. What a haven for anyone who loved to envelop themselves in a story.

Olivia whistled between her teeth as she ran her fingers over the spines and reviewed titles. "You weren't kidding, were you? Nice collection."

A dreamy look swirled in Anna's eyes as she picked a book off the shelf. "I'm going to read every one. You can be anywhere you want to be if you have a story to take you there."

Right. Like a fantasy of moving into a pink dollhouse house with the neighborhood girls. Would they all wake up from this dream and hear their mothers calling them home to supper?

Olivia tapped the spine of a book with an interesting red cover, then picked it up. She hadn't had time to read, hadn't even held a book since her mother died. Was it possible her life could turn back to the old days when there was time for daydreaming and recreational reading—for that matter, recreation of any type?

That reminded her. She needed a job. "So, what did you do over at Nick's today? Was it something I can help with tomorrow?"

Anna hugged her book to her chest. "I don't see why not. We were just weeding in the garden. It's easy, but it's your first week. You don't have to do anything except get comfortable right now. Didn't anyone tell you?"

After sliding the book onto the shelf, Olivia tucked her hands in her back pockets. "Yes, although I'd prefer to get started right away. The last thing I want is to lose my room because I can't come up with the rent."

With a shrug, Anna walked toward the door. "Suit yourself. If it were me, though, I'd enjoy your time off. After all, how often do you just get to relax these days?"

As Olivia started to leave, she couldn't help but reach out and take the red-covered book. It wouldn't hurt to take a break in the evenings and read. At least tonight. Tomorrow she could focus on getting that job.

As they walked back down the hallway toward the stairs, a thump came from behind one of the closed doors. "Did you hear that? It sounded like something heavy fell over."

Anna scooted back and knocked on the door they'd passed. "Lilly? Ruby? You two okay?"

At first, silence was the only response, but as Anna rapped louder, a moan emanated from behind the door.

"I'm coming in! You'd better have clothes on." She turned the knob and pushed open the door.

They found two young teenagers. One with light-brunette hair lying on a purple-covered twin bed, eyes closed, head dangling unnaturally off the edge. The other with dark-brown hair sprawled on the floor, moaning. Anna dropped to her knees beside the girl on the floor. "Ruby! What's wrong?"

Olivia went to the girl still on the bed and checked her pulse. The girl was alive, but she didn't respond to Olivia's hand on her neck. "She's not dead, but she's breathing pretty shallow."

Anna sprang off the floor, her eyes wild. "Stay with them.

I'm going to get help."

9

Chapter Nine

Anna ran out of the room while Olivia kneeled beside the girl on the floor. Wait—the girl was mumbling, not moaning.

"Clouds… fluff–f–fy clouds. Flying."

The girl's eyelids fluttered as if she wanted to open them but was too tired or knocked out.

Olivia hurried back to the second girl and checked for signs of life again. The teen's chest rose and fell. But her eyelids remained closed, and she still didn't react to Olivia's touch. What was going on with these two?

The room displayed all the trappings of a teenager's life. Sequins joined with bright colors to adorn the bedspreads and pillows, and sparkles flickered on the shag rug like someone had woven it with tinsel.

At a loss for how to help, she paced to the door, then to the window to see if anyone was coming to assist. Rapid stomping up the stairs told her she wouldn't be alone with them much longer.

Anna ran back into the room with Nick right behind her. As

soon as he was in, he checked each girl's pulse, then blew out a breath as if relieved.

Why in the world did he look *relieved*?

He patted Anna's shoulder. "It's okay. They're just a little high. Nothing to be concerned about. Let's just get them tucked in until they come down."

Wait… They were high? How did he know? *Why* did he know?

He lifted the girl off the floor and carried her over to the empty bed. Instead of sliding her under the covers, he left her on top and folded the bedspread over her, like she was the filling to a human taco, laying on her side, facing the door.

Next, he went to the teen in the other bed, pushed her head onto the bed, and enfolded her in the covers in the same position. "Come on. They're fine. Let them sleep it off."

Olivia's heart hadn't stopped hammering, and his actions made her more anxious instead of relieved. "You're just going to leave them here? What if they stop breathing or something?"

Having never indulged in any illegal substances, she knew little about how to care for someone who was high. Before the collapse, her parents would have grounded her for life if she'd ever even smelled like weed, much less came home intoxicated.

When she followed him, tears flowed down Anna's face as she stood holding the doorframe for support. Nick tugged Anna into a hug. "Hey, now. It's nothing to cry about. They just wanted to try a buzz. It's no big deal. They're just relaxed and enjoying the ride."

How could he be so blasé about this? Had *he* given them something? Olivia was almost too afraid to ask—*almost*. "Nick, where did they get drugs?"

He smiled at her while he kept an arm around Anna's

shoulders. "That's how I know they're okay. They got a sample from me. It's a safe source. You might like to try a trip yourself. I've heard it's quite a rush."

A weight settled in the pit of Olivia's stomach. Was Nick trying to get them hooked on drugs? Was that why he'd brought them all here? But what would he gain from that?

The hair on the back of her neck rose to attention. "No thanks. I'm good."

Nick's hands went into the air, palms forward. "I'm not trying to pressure you into anything. I don't take them myself. Prefer to stay in control." He chuckled. "These two were just curious. Who am I to stand in their way of seeing if they liked it?"

The two girls, now cocooned in their frilly bedspreads, needed someone mature enough to guide them *away* from dangerous recreation, as her mother always had. As her father did before he fell apart. Before Mom died.

The last thing they needed was Nick's anything-goes attitude.

"We can't leave them like this." Anna's comment came out as a hiccupping sob.

With a rough rub and then a shake to Anna's shoulder, Nick pulled her out into the hallway. "Oh, stop it. I'm telling you. They're fine. Come on, Olivia. Let's head downstairs. We'll talk about the rent arrangements."

The mention of the rent drew her attention away from the sleeping girls and back to her problems. She needed to figure out how to pay for her room. Even if she decided this wasn't where she wanted to be permanently, she'd need work.

Anna wiped her nose on her T-shirt. "If it's all right with you, I'll go wash my face."

Nick nodded, and she scampered toward the bathroom.

With a wave toward the stairs, Nick ushered Olivia down to the living room. Emlyn sat on the overstuffed couch as if she'd been waiting for them. Olivia joined her. Nick slid into the armchair across from the couch, relaxing back, and crossed his legs, poised without a care.

How could he dismiss the two girls upstairs so easily? She leaned into Emlyn. Her new friend smiled at the connection, and between that grin and the warmth from her friend's body, Olivia calmed.

Nick pressed the fingers of his hands together before his chest, creating a tent. "I'm not sure what kind of work you two are used to, but I can help you find something. You're free to relax this first week, Olivia, but since I was going to ask Emlyn to take on a task tomorrow, I thought you might like to join her."

Emlyn jittered her feet, pleading in her eyes. Of course, Olivia would help the girl out. Even though they'd just met, she already liked her new roommate. If they were going to be friends, she needed to show she was a team player. "Of course. I'd love to help any way I can."

"Excellent." Nick clapped. "Just show up in the garden behind my house tomorrow morning early as you can, and we'll get you started."

«»

The sky was starting to release the stars to the sun when Olivia woke the next morning. Her head pounded from lack of sleep. Rambling thoughts hadn't let her brain rest.

What had she gotten into? If she didn't stay here and accept Nick's work, how would she survive? Was Nick just misguided, or was he some sort of drug pusher? And what about her new roommates? Emlyn was so sweet, and Anna and Brandy seemed normal enough. But two of the roommates had questionable ethics, and the other two took drugs. That didn't make for the cozy home she hoped for.

And yet, what other options did she have? The Worthingtons' home wasn't safe for her. Who knew if Rob would follow through on his threat or if he was just blowing smoke in his inebriated condition? So going back to live with her extended family wasn't safe, either. At least this house was clean, maintained, and well furnished.

No. This was her chance for independence, and she wasn't going to let this opportunity slip away. After all, it wasn't as if anyone here had threatened her life. If trusting Nick was what it took for her to live on her own, then she'd have confidence in him… for now.

A knock on her door brought her back to her current situation.

"Come in."

Her butterfly bun in place, Emlyn poked her head in with the opening of the door. "Ready?"

Olivia threw the covers off her bed and shuffled toward her dresser. "Just give me two shakes of a lamb's tail, and I'll be ready."

Emlyn's giggle chimed. "I'll be down at the front door waiting for you."

They grabbed some dried beef on their way through the kitchen. By the time Nick arrived, carrying a stack of bushel baskets, they were waiting just inside the garden gate. "Morning, ladies. We're taking produce to the market today."

He set the baskets down, six in all. "Just load one basket each of cantaloupe, broccoli, cabbage, pumpkin, watermelon, and sweet potatoes. I'll drop you off at the market as soon as you've got it ready to go."

Emlyn fluttered between the baskets and the vegetable rows, but for the first time in a long time, Olivia felt at home. This was just like the work she used to help with at the Worthington farm.

She gave Emlyn a gentle punch on the arm and a huge grin. "We've got it. I've done this plenty of times."

How fortunate they'd started early. Heat wouldn't be an issue at this hour. She began in the watermelon row. This type produced smaller melons, not too heavy. She kneeled beside the first plant while Emlyn goggled, wide-eyed.

"Tell you what. These are easy to harvest." Olivia lifted the first ripe-looking melon and thumped it with her knuckle. "Hear that? Sounds hollow. That means it's ripe. Just twist it while you hold the vine. That way you won't break the plant."

The fruit broke off, and Olivia tucked it into the bushel basket. "You harvest these, and I'll go work on the broccoli. Sound good?"

"Got it. Thanks." Emlyn's relieved smile promised she understood the assignment, but Olivia watched her pick up the next melon, thump it, and then twist it off the vine. "I can do this, no problem."

The hour it took to fill the baskets went much too quickly. Olivia could work in the garden all day. As nature soothed her soul, she missed being amongst plants.

Once they'd moved the overflowing containers outside the garden gate, they went to the back door to let Nick know they were ready for a ride to the market.

Nadine answered their knock as if she'd been waiting for them. Anger flashed over her face, but why? "I'll tell him you're ready."

No invitation to come in—no warm greeting—just a door closed in their faces. What was her problem? Could she still be upset Olivia had taken the room? Too bad she couldn't understand the confusing messages the woman was sending with her eyes.

The door reopened, and Nick joined them. "I've got the golf cart charged up and ready to go. Follow me."

The long, three-benched golf cart in the garage, almost identical to the one the Worthingtons owned, had become a popular mode of transportation for those who had solar chargers. Though she hadn't seen panels on the main house or their pink palace, that didn't mean they didn't have one some place.

After they loaded the baskets, they were off to the market with Nick giving them instructions as he drove. They were to trade the raw ingredients for as much canned or otherwise preserved food as they could manage.

Nick wasn't poor, so his methods didn't make sense. She scooted forward in her seat to peer over the front bench. "Why don't we preserve the food ourselves? Then we could get more for it."

He flicked sandy-blond hair away from his eyes as he smiled at her over his shoulder. "You are the smart one, aren't you? Yes, we could get more for it. But all our canning jars are full after the summer crop. If you want to barter for some empty ones, Nadine can organize a canning party. Canned pumpkin would make for some wonderful fall recipes."

The drive took more than an hour at the cart's max speed, so they had plenty of time to discuss canning and gardening. Because of her time helping on the farm, she knew as much as, if not more than, Nick did. Poor Emlyn was clueless. That would have to change if she was going to make it in the world these days.

At the edge of the market, they offloaded the baskets at a wooden booth. Nick must have connections to afford a permanent spot. Customers would know where to find his offerings every week, which equated to more traffic and more sales.

The stand wasn't in the same zone as her family's wood business. Still, she fretted they might see her. What would she say if they did? She'd keep an eye out for them… and duck down if any of them came near.

After they arranged the fruits and vegetables on the booth's slanted front, she was ready to get to work. "I'm pretty good at doing the running and drumming up business if you want to man the booth, Emlyn."

"No." Nick's quick, firm response halted her. His frown morphed into a relaxed smile. "I mean, we've got a regular clientele here. They'll be expecting two people at the booth today to handle all the traffic."

What? That was beyond odd. All the vendors sent a second person on walkabout if they had someone available. "You sure? I'm excellent at negotiating."

Nick pointed behind the display counter where Emlyn stood waiting for customers. "I'm positive."

With a shrug, Olivia joined her new friend and stuffed her antsy hands into her pockets. "It's your game."

His grin was almost too big. "Yes. Yes, it is. Thank you for understanding that." He climbed into the cart and turned the key. "I'll be back at the end of the day. My customers are important to me. So, I expect to hear good things from them about how sweet you ladies are today."

And with that, he drove off.

It wasn't like she'd planned to be mean to his customers, but his comment seemed so odd. If his patrons were so important to him, why didn't he want her to drum up more business? She might sneak off after an hour or so anyway, just to show him how she could improve his sales by doing the walkabout.

The sweet scent of the cantaloupes was enticing, especially since the jerky breakfast was wearing off after their hour of harvesting. Too bad she didn't have a knife to slice one open to show their customers the quality of the fruit.

A burly man in jeans, a flannel shirt, and a cowboy hat sauntered to their stand. "Well, hello, ladies. What are you offering this fine morning?"

Olivia waved a hand over the produce as if she were a hostess fawning over a fresh buffet. "Everything you see was just picked this morning. The cantaloupes smell particularly sweet, though."

Picking the nicest one up, she offered it to him.

His eyes roamed over her from head to toe as he ignored the proffered fruit.

"How old are you?"

Caught off guard, she fumbled the cantaloupe, nearly dropping it. "Seventeen?"

One side of his mouth lifted as he then accepted the orb from her hand. "Nice and fresh."

The way he looked at her made her skin crawl. The comment seemed to be about something other than the fruit. Good thing she had the counter between them.

Shaking the creepy feeling out of her head, she picked up another cantaloupe from the display table. "Would you like to purchase or trade for anything we have?"

His grin spread out his fat lips, and he barked out a laugh. "What's your name, girlie?"

Instant flames leaped into her chest, and her heart pounded. This guy wasn't just weird—he was rude and misogynistic. With her fingers curling into fists, she flattened her arms against her sides. Customer or not, she didn't need this person around. "Sir, my name is not girlie, and my job today is to sell this produce. If you aren't interested in what is for sale, then I would kindly ask you to leave."

His eyes widened as if his treatment of women had never resulted in the slap she wanted to provide. He returned the cantaloupe. "Tell Nick Chet stopped by. I'll talk to him about putting in a full order soon."

A shudder ran through her as she watched his retreating back. She hoped she never saw him again.

10

Chapter Ten

Throughout the rest of the day, customers came and went. Olivia and Emlyn did the best they could to sell the produce. Though a lot of women with children stopped by, an unusual number of men came to their booth. All of them were as creepy as the first one. Olivia'd never felt so weirded out at the market.

The hour was getting late, and they hadn't sold even half of what they'd brought. If Nick had been willing to let her roam, she'd have most of the produce gone. She paced as the frustration built.

By the time she'd walked around their booth a dozen times, Emlyn grabbed her arm. "You're making me nervous and dizzy. Why don't you sit and relax? We're almost done here. Nick should be back soon."

Crossing her arms over her chest, Olivia huffed out a breath. "Exactly."

Emlyn's eyes narrowed. "Huh?"

Olivia gestured toward the unsold food. "Don't you get it? We're supposed to work these jobs to help pay our way—to cover the rent. If we can't sell anything, then we aren't making money."

Eyes wide, Emlyn sprang out of her seated position. "I hadn't thought of that. What are we going to do?"

Plans had been swirling around in Olivia's head all day. Did she dare ignore Nick's demand that they both stay put at the booth? If she could sneak a few trips around the market, she could get some sales from her best customers.

A gaggle of children ran through, the little girl trailing with the rag doll. The pixie smiled shyly at Olivia, and she was just about to bend down and call her over when Emlyn hollered. "You get back here with that, ya little thief!"

A boy about eight or nine with dirty hands and face scampered away with a cantaloupe.

Olivia's heart jolted, and she sprinted after him, calling over her shoulder. "Stay here. I'll get him."

Even though her legs were longer and she should have been able to outpace him, the scrappy fellow had experience evading pursuers. As he ran, he slid between people, under tables, and through the tightest spots he could find to slow her pursuit.

She poured all her pent-up frustration into her speed, dodging and weaving every obstacle the boy put in front of her. No way she was going to let him get away from her. *Get back here, you little scamp.*

She was making progress when the boy stopped at a table and darted behind a woman wearing a beige wide-brimmed sun hat. Carissa.

By the time Olivia got to the honey-laden table, she was out of breath and patience. The boy peeked out from behind Carissa's skirt, and Olivia spoke to him in between gasps. "Either give me… back that melon… or pay up… little man."

He buried his head in Carissa's skirts, clutching his ill-gotten gains.

Carissa knelt beside the boy. "Let's see what you've got there."

After a peek at Olivia, he held out the fruit to the older woman.

With a nod, Carissa said, "What a lovely cantaloupe." She leaned in and sniffed. "Smells sweet too. You must be hungry. Did you get any breakfast or lunch today?"

The little guy ogled the melon.

"Hmm. I can see why it might tempt you to steal. But you have to work for what you need. Earn it." She put her hand under the boy's chin and lifted his head to make eye contact. "We've talked about this before. Right?"

A tear slipped down his cheek, and he nodded.

She took the boy by the shoulders and turned his body toward Olivia. "I think you owe this young lady an apology, then."

Olivia barely heard his whispered sorry.

What could she say? She hadn't thought about how hungry he might be. She'd chased him halfway through the market, but now she felt a little queasy. The poor guy was just trying to survive. She knew the feeling.

He held the fruit out to her, but she waved a hand, refusing to take it. "No. It's yours."

Carissa pulled the boy to her side. "Let's negotiate, shall we?"

He blinked up at her, his face scrunching.

She pointed to the bowl of homemade honey candy. "How many pieces of candy, do you think, for one melon?"

Carissa was trying to teach the boy a lesson, so Olivia put a serious look on her face and rubbed her chin as if in thought. "I think perhaps three."

"What do you think, Matthew?" Carissa cupped a hand on the boy's shoulder. "Is that fair?"

He shook his head and waggled two fingers. "Two."

Carissa grinned. "A born negotiator." She tipped her head to Olivia. "You have a counteroffer, my dear."

Olivia couldn't contain her smile as she held her hand out to the boy. "Deal. Shake on it."

Still clasping his melon, he stuck a grimy hand out and shook.

With a clap on the boy's back, Carissa held her hand out to him, and he handed her the fruit. "Now pay the nice lady."

He stepped up to the table, removed two candies from the bowl, and gave them to Olivia.

She tucked them into a pocket. "Thank you."

"Now you need to work to pay for that candy." Carissa ruffled his hair. "And it just so happens that I could use a hand closing and packing away what's left in a few hours. So how about we cut that melon up for you to eat while we're waiting for the end of market hours?"

His eyes lit up, and his grin stretched from ear to ear.

Carissa slipped a knife from a tote, along with a hand towel. She then poured water from a thermos on the towel and wiped some grime off the boy's face and hands before she quartered the melon. After she scooped out the seeds and plopped them in a ramekin, she placed the quarters on the towel and gestured for the boy to dig in.

He chomped at the fruit.

Carissa spoke, pulling Olivia's attention away from the boy's feeding frenzy. "If I recall correctly, your name is Olivia. Yes?"

"Yes." She returned the smile. "It's nice to see you again. Sorry it's under these circumstances, though."

"No matter. God has a way of bringing people together in

his own time—in unusual ways too." The honey vendor wiped her now-sticky hands on another towel. "I hadn't seen any of your family today selling firewood. I hope all is well."

What could Olivia say to that? Exposing her family drama didn't seem right. She owed them that much, at least. "I'm not positive how they are. I moved out on my own."

Carissa's eyebrows went up. "Really? How exciting! You seem a little young to be on your own though. Is everything all right?"

If only she could tell her, but Mom always said family business was private. "Sure. We're good. My cousin isn't doing so well, so I am trying to leave one less mouth to feed. You know, striking out on my own."

Carissa reached across the table and touched Olivia's arm. "There are a lot of dangers out there for a young lady. If you ever need a friend, you can always come to me. Remember that for me, will you?"

The gesture was so sweet and so genuine. A tear sprang into Olivia's eye, and she had to swallow hard to keep a sob from escaping. Maybe she had a friend in this woman. Time to put the offer to the test. "You said you'd be willing to teach me about beekeeping. I'd be happy to work for you, just for the sake of learning—and for some of your honey. If you can spare it."

With a crisp nod, Carissa pulled her tote onto the table and rummaged in it before coming up with a pencil. "I thought you'd never ask."

She picked up a jar of honey and wrote an address on the white label, just above the drawing of a bee. Then she handed it to Olivia. "I live not too far out of town between Manchester and Warm Springs. Could you make it out this week?"

The address was a main road. It wouldn't be hard to find. Olivia was used to walking, so getting there wouldn't be a problem if she started early. If just showing up was all she needed to do to get a job, she was all in. "I'll be there."

A slurping sound drew their attention back to Matthew. He'd devoured all four of the melon sections, leaving only the thinnest shell of the outer skin on the towel. The noise came from his attempt to chew every bit of flesh from the rind.

Carissa motioned for him to use the damp towel to clean his face and hands again, and he complied, still staring at the melon remains.

Oops. Olivia had left the booth and roamed well out-of-bounds. The last thing she needed was to get caught not tending to Nick's food stand. "I need to get back to work. I'll see you later this week. Okay?"

"See you then."

As she headed back, she thought about the bees and honey. Too bad she couldn't get one without the other. Few people sold honey at the market, so there was plenty of opportunity there. And, with her negotiating skills, she'd do well. But the bees frightened her. She'd been stung a few times—who hadn't? The worst was as a child when she'd stepped on a bee while running in the backyard.

Cringing, she rubbed at the shivers rising on her arms. It had been a birthday party, her own. Her cousin was there to celebrate, and they'd been playing in the pool. She'd had to go to the bathroom but didn't want to take the time to find her shoes. That's when she'd stepped on the bee. A smile tugged at her lips. Dad had done a silly dance and thrown himself into the pool with his clothes on to get her to stop crying. It had worked.

She was still smiling when the vegetable stand came into view. Nick was there, legs crossed and hands in his jeans pockets. He leaned back against the front of the booth, looking grim. He'd seen her coming, and his eyes bored into her as she got closer.

Emlyn stood behind the stand display, her arms wrapped around her waist and gaze darting between Nick and Olivia.

Well, this didn't look good.

He'd told her not to leave the stand. But she hadn't gone just to walk about. He'd understand.

With a plastered-on smile, she held up the jar of honey as she arrived. "Good news. I think I found a job."

He pushed away from the booth, looming taller than she remembered. "I thought my instructions had been clear. Was there some confusion on your part as to what staying put meant?"

She looked past Nick to her friend, but Emlyn wouldn't make eye contact. "It's not like I meant to leave. I chased a thief. Didn't Emlyn tell you?"

Advancing toward her, he grabbed her arm. "You think I care about some little brat snatching a piece of fruit? I gave you a direct order."

The pressure on her biceps, though not painful, was terrifyingly possessive. She tried to wrench free, but he tightened his hold.

"I'm sorry. I did what I thought was best in the situation. Look." She raised the honey jar with her opposite hand. "I got payment and then some—an entire jar of honey for one cantaloupe—and a job working with bees on top of that."

Nick closed his eyes and sucked in loud breaths, releasing each one slower than the one before. When he opened his eyes again, he dropped her arm and spoke in a soothing tone.

"It's not good for a young girl to be milling about the market by herself. I'm just trying to keep you safe." He stepped back and waved toward Emlyn. "And I thought you two were friends. Weren't you the least bit concerned about abandoning your coworker?"

One look at her friend revealed pooled tears in Emlyn's eyes.

Rats. Olivia hadn't meant to scare anyone. Now she felt like a real jerk. "I'm sorry." Then she nudged her friend. "Sorry, Emlyn."

Emlyn turned away while swiping at her eyes.

Nick draped his arm around Olivia's shoulders and drew her in close so he could speak in low tones directly into her ear. "We have rules for a reason. Everyone remains alive and well, and there's no confusion when everyone follows the rules. You wouldn't want to end up on the street now, would you?"

Her heart dropped into her stomach. Surely, he wouldn't kick her out over something as stupid as this. "No. I like the pink house."

Stepping toward the vegetable stand, he tugged her along. "And we enjoy having you with us."

She wanted to feel relieved by those words, but they felt more ominous than friendly.

Once they were behind the stall's presentation table, he pushed her to arm's length and met her eye. "Look." He jerked his thumb to Emlyn. "You made her cry. Friends don't do that to each other, do they?"

Olivia's throat closed as she ducked her head. She wrapped her arms around her waist, still clutching the honey. "No. They don't."

He gripped her chin, forcing eye contact. "We've learned a

valuable lesson today, haven't we?"

She tried to nod, but his hand on her chin prevented full movement. "Yes."

He smiled as if it were one of the happiest moments of his life, instead of having won a disagreement. "Excellent. But to make sure we're clear, you won't be eating supper tonight. I'd say you didn't earn a meal with having pulled that stunt. Don't you agree?"

After he freed her chin, she managed a nod.

11

Chapter Eleven

Surreal. It was as if she was ten years old again and Mom had sent her to bed without supper. Except it was her landlord. Was this happening? No. Sure, Nick had just been angry, but this was America. Land of the free and home of the brave. Adults didn't hand out juvenile punishments to other fully-grown people. Regardless of her seventeen years of age, she was on her own here. She intended to eat supper.

She didn't say another word as they packed up the vegetable stand and drove home. Once they'd unloaded the golf cart, she returned to the pink house with Emlyn and showered to wash the day away. Unfortunately, the power wasn't on today, so the water was cool. No long soak, just a quick in-and-out cleansing.

As she dressed, she heard the girls downstairs—time to meet the rest of her housemates. She wiggled into her socks and cringed at another unpleasant surprise when her big toe broke through the thinning material.

Lovely. She hated darning socks—and who knew if anyone here even had a needle and thread she could borrow? Leaving her toe hanging out, she padded down the hallway and stairs and headed for the source of the noise in the kitchen.

The moment she stepped into view, the chatter ceased, and all eyes turned in her direction. A mixture of emotions greeted her—few of them warm and welcoming.

Emlyn sat on the first stool at the counter. Her eyes reflected something like sorrow, even though she gave a weak smile. "Hey, everyone, this is Olivia."

A tall woman, perhaps a smidgen under six feet, with long, straight red hair, gazed at her. About twenty years old, she munched on a carrot. "Heard you already ticked Nick off. Good job."

Emlyn hopped off her stool, walked over to Olivia, and hugged her. Then she faced the group with Olivia at her side. "That's Molly with the carrot. And I don't think you've met Stella, Lilly, and Ruby. At least not while Lilly and Ruby were conscious." She gave a timid laugh.

Stella said nothing as Olivia's eyes met hers. She turned her back on Olivia and walked to the cabinet to get something.

Lilly and Ruby appeared healthier than last time she'd seen them. Both sat at the kitchen island with steaming bowls of pinto beans. Lilly made eye contact, then became absorbed in her food. Ruby grinned like a little kid, feet swinging back and forth as she twirled a spoon in her hand. "Nice to meet you, Olivia."

At least one of them was friendly.

Anna and Brandy avoided Olivia. One at a time, they scooped a serving of pinto beans from the steaming pot on the stove.

Nadine stood by the stove, arms crossed and eyes narrowed. She picked up a lid and slammed it down on the pot. "You shouldn't even be in the kitchen tonight."

With that, everyone except Nadine and Emlyn turned away from Olivia as if she were painful to look at. Unreal.

A squeeze of her shoulder reminded her Emlyn was still beside her. "Nadine brought dinner over tonight, but I'm not all that hungry, anyway. Want to check out the library?"

Without a response, Olivia headed back up the stairs, Emlyn trailing with an oil lamp. Nadine shouted from behind them. "Don't think you're going to sneak back here and get food, missy. You're cut off."

In the library, Emlyn pulled a short carrot from her pocket and held it out to Olivia. "I snuck you one while Nadine wasn't watching."

Olivia batted the carrot away. "What is going on here? Since when does Nick control me? And what right does Nadine have to say who eats and who doesn't?"

Slipping the vegetable back into her pocket, Emlyn shrugged and stepped under the window. She tapped at the glass, the world dark beyond. "I know what you mean. It was Stella's turn to cook, but Nadine showed up with the pot and said Nick sent her to enforce the house rules."

House rules? Olivia didn't recall hearing anything about food privileges related to house rules. "We're renters, not children. Who ever heard of cutting a renter off from eating when they broke a house rule?"

Emlyn's reflection on the glass must have been fascinating because she couldn't take her eyes off it. "But we aren't really renters yet, are we? At least I'm not. I haven't paid anything, only did that one job for Nick so far, and even then, we didn't sell all that much, did we?"

Rats. Emlyn was right. Neither of them had paid anything for living here, much less for food. When Nick offered her a place to live, he'd never said food would be part of the deal. Meals were a bonus she hadn't expected, so why was she getting all bent out of shape because he wasn't giving her a free meal tonight?

Her stomach rumbled with an audible gurgle. "I'm sorry. You shouldn't have skipped out on supper because of me. I'm going to be fine. It's not like I've been eating regularly for the past couple of years. Skipping a meal won't kill me."

When Emlyn flitted to her side and proffered the carrot once more, Olivia accepted it with a smile. "Thanks. Why don't you go on down and get yourself some supper? I need time by myself to process things, anyway."

"You sure?" Emlyn set down the oil lamp and glanced at the door. "I hate to leave you alone with just a carrot."

Olivia gave her friend's shoulder a playful shove toward the hall. "I'm fine. Go on."

"Well, only because you insist." Emlyn scooted toward the door. "I am hungry after being at the market all day. The popcorn vendor was within sniffing distance. I'll see if I can sneak you another carrot—or six."

"Please, don't get in trouble because of me. I'll be fine."

After Emlyn left, Olivia fell into a chair next to the bookcase and bit into the carrot. Munching sounds filled her ears as her teeth chewed through the crisp vegetable. Unfortunately, the moment it was gone, she wanted more. Instead of filling the void, it seemed to accentuate the emptiness.

Why did it seem as if the world were against her some days? It was as if she had the reverse Midas touch. She giggled at the term. Until this moment, she'd forgotten about school lessons. Before the world fell apart, one of her English teachers had insisted they all learn about Greek myths. King Midas had the gift of turning anything he touched into gold. It had seemed a blessing until he turned his beloved daughter into gold as well. Oops.

Not her, though. Instead of turning her world into gold, she had the opposite effect. Everything she touched fell apart. If they attached her name to a project—expect failure. No, not failure—utter destruction.

With a sigh, she stepped up to the bookshelf and ran her fingers over the nearest spines. There were some classics here. *Atlas Shrugged* rested within reach. She'd started reading the book in school, but never finished it. Perhaps she should try to finish it again.

On the bottom shelf, she noticed a black, leather-bound Bible, the NIV version. Memories of her mother came to mind. Mom had three or four translations of the book, but the NIV was her favorite. How many times had Olivia come down the stairs in the morning to find Mom reading her Bible as she drank her morning coffee? Often, she'd share the passage she was reading with Olivia, and they'd discuss what it meant.

A warm feeling spread through Olivia's chest when she hefted the book from the shelf. She thumbed through the pages, looking for a passage she knew by heart—not because of her own interest, but because it was Mom's favorite Bible verse. There had been an enormous stencil of the verse on the living room wall—Mom's handiwork. She wished she could touch that old wall. No. Forget the wall. She wished she could hug Mom.

Acts... Romans... First and Second Corinthians... Galatians. Page flip... flip... flip... Chapter five. There it was. She whispered the words aloud. " 'It is for freedom that Christ has set us free. Stand firm, then, and do not let yourselves be burdened again by a yoke of slavery.' "

She could have quoted the words without looking, but somehow seeing them was like having Mom beside her once more.

Mom had grown up in a strict church. She'd told Olivia stories of having her hair length measured by the youth pastor and of kids being kicked out of the youth group for various rule infractions. When she'd explained her love for this verse to Olivia, Mom had given her a glimpse into her past.

"I know the verse is really about legalism, and the apostle Paul is admonishing people not to get trapped by the old rules of Judaism. But it means more than that to me," Mom had said. "It means freedom from the people who wanted to confine and control me. I'll never let that happen again."

What would Mom say about what was happening now to her daughter? Olivia didn't even need to think twice about it. Mom would say she should go find herself some supper and a new place to live. Of course, Mom also hadn't survived the variant. If she had, Olivia wouldn't be in this predicament.

"I miss you, Mom," she said to the empty room.

She'd made her decision. She wasn't going to hide in this little library. She'd find her big-girl panties and some supper. She was hungry.

After putting the Bible back onto the shelf, she marched downstairs.

She passed Emlyn on the stairs. "Nadine is still there." Emlyn ducked her head, her bun slipping forward. "She packed the food up awfully fast."

Olivia touched her friend's shoulder. "Did you get to eat?"

"Some." Emlyn let out a little laugh. "Never swallowed so fast in my life. It's going to sit like a rock in my stomach tonight. I just know it."

Olivia's stomach sunk at the thought of costing her friend a meal. "Sorry."

"It's okay. I'm going to head to bed. G'night."

"'Night."

Olivia's agitation spiked. This was insane. She couldn't let her friends go hungry because of her. Something had to be done… or at least said. She continued to the kitchen. Nadine was still there, talking in low tones to Stella, who was placing a freshly washed dish into the cabinet. Both froze when Olivia entered the room. Silence hung as heavy as a sodden towel over a drying line.

"Gotta go." Stella draped the dish towel over the edge of the sink. "I have a date tonight."

With a glare toward Olivia, the older girl strode out of the room.

"What's your problem?" Olivia asked Stella's retreating form. When Stella kept moving with no response, Olivia stepped closer to Nadine. "And what gives with you?"

With a dismissive huff, Nadine retrieved the pot holding the remnants of supper and started toward the door. "I told you not to come here. Didn't I?"

As if that explained anything.

The frustration building inside Olivia was near to exploding, but she needed to remain calm if she wanted information. She drew in a slow, deep breath and then released it to a count of five. Forcing calm into her tone, she blocked the other woman's exit. "Yes. You tried to keep me from moving here. But I didn't have much choice. It was that or living under a tree someplace. Would you like to explain what's going on?"

"No way you can be that naïve. Can't you see Nick wants to control you? You think I enjoy what I do for that man?" She lifted the pot. "Keeping you from eating is the beginning. You don't want to know what's next."

Those drugged girls… Was that his plan for her? Did he want to get all of them addicted? But if that were the case, wouldn't all the girls look high all the time? They didn't. It had just been that one time. "What does he want?"

Nadine rolled her eyes, but as she opened her mouth, the front door opened. "Good evening, ladies. Who's home?"

Nick. What was he doing here?

Rushing past her, Nadine whispered, "Get out."

Nick came around the corner into the kitchen and grabbed Nadine's arm before she could escape. "How'd supper go? Any problems?"

Nadine's jaw flexed, her chin dipping as she stood frozen in place by his grip. Her face flushed. "Fine. No trouble."

"Excellent." He maintained his hold. "And if I asked the ladies, I'd find you followed my instructions?"

Features still taut and red, she nodded. "Of course."

He paused as if sizing up the situation. Then he removed his hand from her arm with a dramatic flip of his fingers in the air. "I'll see you back at the house in a few, then."

The moment she was free, she strode to the front door and exited without another comment or a look back.

Leaning against the kitchen island, he crossed his arms over his chest and addressed Olivia. "Let's talk about today's events. Shall we?"

Oh yes, please. She was ready for this. "You don't own me."

His eyebrows rose while he twisted his lips into a smug smile. "I never said I did. But do you expect to live here for free? Am

I running some sort of charity here?"

Now they were getting back to the original question. What would the rent cost her? "I never asked for a handout. I told you I'd gotten a job. Just tell me what I owe, and I'll get to work on it."

With a laugh, he said, "Ah yes, you said you'd gotten a job. Honey curator, I believe?"

Now he was making fun of her.

"It's as good a job as any. Honey is a hot commodity, and few people sell it at the market. I could do well."

He uncrossed his arms and entered her personal space. Using his height to full advantage, he got close enough that she had to look up into his eyes. The room felt too small with him this close. She tried to back away, but he'd blocked her against a chair she hadn't realized was behind her. "You might. Or you might not."

If he thought he was going to intimidate her, he had another thought coming. Glaring up at him, she clenched her hands into fists. She lengthened her spine to gain her maximum five-foot height. "I will."

They stood there as if a battle of the wills were taking place. Who would look away first? Certainly, not her.

His breath felt cool against her flushed face before he let out a huff and backed away. "Try your experiment. We'll see how it goes."

She wanted to spit at him as he walked back toward the door. Perhaps next time she would.

Chapter Twelve

The rumble in Olivia's stomach morphed into a hollow feeling as she got out of bed before dawn. Sure, she'd gone without a meal before, but that didn't make the experience any more pleasant. After Nick left the night before, she'd searched the kitchen for something to eat but hadn't found anything. She'd eaten the two honey candies, but they turned out to be more of a tease than anything.

How weird to find a kitchen with no food in it. As sparse as her cousin's family had lived, even they had some basics. But there wasn't a scrap of leftover vegetables to scrounge, as if someone had purposely taken anything edible out of the house.

She pulled her socks and shoes on, got her backpack out of her closet, and headed for the kitchen. Water sloshed into her thermoses from the kitchen faucet as she filled them. Once done, she gave the room one more quick search in case she'd missed something the night before. No, still nothing to eat.

After putting her day's water supply into her backpack, she filled a glass from the tap. She chugged the full serving, then a second, stopping only when she couldn't drink anymore. Her stomach sloshed as she headed toward the door, but it felt better than an empty belly.

On the porch, the sound of night was in the buzz of insects surrounding her. Strolling in the dark wasn't ideal, but she wanted to be as far down the road as possible before the sun rose and people got busy. Carissa's place wasn't far by prevariant standards, but when you had to walk the whole way, it could take a while. She'd be avoiding the roads, so the trip would take even longer.

She estimated her destination somewhere between five and eight miles. A brisk walk, weaving in and out of the woods, should take a couple of hours—plenty of time to think.

Power was out. Good thing the moon brightened the sky to keep her from walking in complete darkness. Streetlights used to be such a convenience in cities and towns. Flashlights supplemented, but who had batteries these days? Not her. The supply chain collapse had seemingly sent them all back a century in progress. The rich could still find some of these items. Money always found a way.

When the sidewalks ended, she slipped into the woods and skirted the edge. Every crackling branch or crunching sound raised the hairs on the back of her neck. Was this a smart move on her part?

Being alone stunk… big time. Why hadn't her parents had a second child? What she wouldn't give for a sister to walk beside her. The thought brought a fresh ache to her chest. Mom would have marched right beside her. Dad would never have allowed her out in the dark on her own to tromp through the woods. At least not before he started drinking. Before the world fell apart. Before the collapse.

Perhaps she should have asked Emlyn to come with her, but

then again, the job offer was for her. It wouldn't have been fair to ask her new friend to take this long walk just so she wouldn't be alone.

An hour into her trip, she felt light-headed. If only she'd kept that jar of honey instead of turning it in to Nick. It had been worth more than the single cantaloupe she'd claimed she traded it for. That would teach her to appease a man. It hadn't helped, anyway.

By the time Carissa's mailbox came into view, nausea overtook Olivia, and she felt close to dry heaves. One of her thermoses was already empty from her attempts to subdue the hunger.

Relieved to find the house just behind a row of privacy trees, she trudged up the driveway to an adorable, single-story, white home with a wraparound porch and solar panels on the roof. The moment she reached the front door, she knocked, hoping Carissa would be awake.

She'd moved to take refuge on a porch swing when the door opened and Carissa's warm smile beamed at her. "I was hoping to see you soon." Then her smile faded, and she reached out to steady Olivia. "You don't look so good. Come in and sit for a spell."

She barely took in the furnishings as she tottered after the other woman. Everything looked well worn, but comfortable, as if the owner had lived in it for decades with little change. A sweet smell in the home grew stronger as they walked. Then, in the kitchen, jars lined the white-tile counter. Dark honey half-filled one on the end. A tall, three-legged, silver container with a spout stood on the counter as well.

Everything about the room, with its cheery yellow walls and white cabinets and white-tiled counters, backsplash, and flooring, was bright and airy. As if nothing dark or oppressive had ever threatened its haven. Her mind relaxed, and her stomach growled in response to the sights and smells. She wobbled on her feet as Carissa eyed her. Carissa rushed over to the country table, pulled a chair out, and pushed it behind Olivia's knees, forcing her to sit.

What a relief to collapse into it.

Carissa went to the counter and slid the half-filled jar under the spigot of the silver container and started the flow of honey into the jar. "Care for a bite to eat? I was just about to have a late breakfast."

"Sure. How can I help?" Olivia had every intention of standing, but her body didn't want to cooperate. Instead, she ended up on the edge of the wooden chair, hand on the nearby table. "I'm not great in the kitchen, but I can manage the basics."

After she screwed on the lid, Carissa lifted the filled jar to the light coming through the yellow curtains swagged over the kitchen window. "Can't ask for better than nature's sweetest, can you?" She placed the bottled sunshine in the line of filled ones. "Ever had grits with honey? I used to love it with milk, but it's so hard to keep milk these days, even if you can get it."

"We usually use molasses. When we can afford it, that is."

"You're in for a treat, then."

With the clatter of pots and pans, Carissa gathered a saucepan, then opened a cabinet to reveal jars of corn grits, flour, homemade candies, and honey. She selected the grits, then measured them into the pan along with water and a shake of what must have been salt. "What do you say we chat while this heats?"

Olivia pointed to the line of containers. "How long does it take bees to make that much honey?"

Carissa's silky ebony hair swished as she continued to stir the grits. "It takes two to three weeks and about five hundred and fifty bees to make a pound of honey. It all depends on how many flowers are in the area, how well established the colony is, and how the weather cooperates."

"How many bees do you have?"

"You'll see. There's an orchard behind the house where I keep the hives. I've not counted them in a while, but there are quite a few out there."

More audible gurgling emanated from Olivia's stomach, and she grabbed it. If only she could crawl underneath the table. "Sorry. I missed supper last night and left before breakfast."

No need to go into details. No one wanted to sound pathetic.

With a swirl of the pan's contents, Carissa tapped the wooden spoon on the edge, then set the spoon on a saucer beside the stove. "It's almost done."

She gathered bowls from a cabinet, scooped grits into them, and poured a generous dollop of honey on top. After retrieving spoons from a drawer, she set one and a steaming bowl in front of Olivia.

"Thank you."

"Quite welcome." Carissa sank onto the chair across from her and scooped her long hair behind her back. "Remember, it's hot."

Olivia was about to take her first bite when Carissa held out a hand to her.

Oh.

Olivia hadn't done this since her mother had been alive.

Accepting the outstretched hand, she bowed her head as Carissa prayed. "Father, thank you for this food and for the company you've brought me. Please guide our work today to honor you. Amen."

"Amen." The word tasted foreign. Olivia scooped a spoonful of grits and licked them off the spoon. "Hot… hot… hot." She waved a hand in front of her mouth and huffed in and out to cool the burn.

Carissa winked. "Told you."

Olivia had gotten the mouthful cool enough to swallow, then blew on the next spoonful before indulging. "What does a beekeeper do? I've never known anyone who raised them before. All I can think of is roping them with an itsy-bitsy lasso."

Carissa's laughter was the full-belly version. A beautiful sound. "Today, we'll check to see which hives need another super." Olivia's confusion must have been obvious because Carissa's sun-kissed cheeks lifted with her smile. "That means another layer on top of their hive so they can make more honey."

Never having seen a hive before, Olivia could only picture the books from her childhood. The silly bear who stole honey from the bees because he loved it so much. Those hives looked like huge gray balls hanging from trees. So just how were they going to add a layer to something like that?

Her bowl was empty before she knew it. She'd scraped every grain out. Setting the spoon down gently, she wished there was more. But her shrunken stomach felt maxed out. "Thank you again. It was wonderful with honey."

Carissa rose, collected both bowls, and set them in the kitchen sink. "Come on. We'll get you a bee suit, though I presume you have been stung before and aren't allergic, right?"

"Right." When Olivia stood, she felt tired, but less so than before eating. She followed Carissa into a mudroom at the back of the house. White jackets hung on pegs.

Each of the coverings had strange hoods with nets that zipped onto the collars. Carissa helped her get the jacket on and the hood secured over her head. Gloves that rolled up over her hands and forearms and her elbows came next. Elastic secured them in the cocoon.

They went out the back door and walked toward an orchard, the air heady with the sweet aroma of apples ripening. There had to be dozens of rows and more apples than she could eat in a lifetime hanging from their branches.

In between the fruit trees, white boxes stood on metal legs. Bees flew in and out of a long opening at the bottom of the hive. Olivia stepped back, her heart racing.

Carissa held a metal container with a funneled metal top. After lifting the lid, she lit a match and dropped it into the container, then closed it. With a squeeze, she pumped a bellow on the side, and smoke puffed out the top. "It's okay. You're fine. Come on over, and you can work the smoker."

Well, this was it. Did she want the job or not?

Olivia stiffened, thinking of Nick's angry eyes and the night without food. Yes. She wanted this job—*no matter what.* Holding out her hand toward the smoldering container, she joined Carissa.

As she surrendered the smoker, Carissa said, "Squeeze it occasionally to keep the fire going. Be careful. It gets hot."

Carissa walked up to the hive and waved Olivia closer. "When I lift the lid, puff some smoke into it. It sends the bees to the bottom of the box."

The buzzing intensity increased as Carissa lifted the lid, so Olivia puffed smoke at the hive as fast as she could.

Carissa laughed. "Slowly. That's enough. You'll choke us

too if you're not careful." Setting the lid against the hive, she wiggled a section of the box out. Honeycomb in various stages of completion filled the frame. "Looks like they're almost done with this one. We'll add another layer."

While Olivia watched, Carissa went into a nearby shed, then returned with a wooden four-sided box, open on either end, but with empty frames lining it. She settled it on top of the hive, then put the lid back in place. Turning to Olivia, she smiled. "See? Easy-peasy. Right? Now we just need to check them all."

The rest of the day, Olivia followed her new employer around the orchard, manning the smoker. By the time the sun was giving way, her fear had given way into fascination. She wanted her own orchard with bees someday.

That evening, as she walked back home, her shoulders ached with the weight of her bag. This time, not only did she have water for the walk but also jars of honey and plenty of apples.

Carissa was more than generous and hadn't taken no for an answer when Olivia said she was paying too much for a day's labor. At this rate, she could cover her rent and then some. Next time she talked to Nick about rent, she'd be prepared to pay him in liquid gold.

Walking back up the sidewalk to the pink house, she was happy to see the lights on. Maybe the power would stay on long enough for her to get a book out of the library and read a chapter or two.

She found the front door locked—not unexpected, but she didn't have a key. Why hadn't she thought of asking for one? No matter. She knocked. When the door opened, Stella stood there grimacing, her top too revealing and her skirt almost nonexistent. "Decided to come back, huh? Couldn't find a better place?"

They must have thought she'd left when she wasn't there this morning. She should have thought to let Emlyn know or at least written a note. "I just went to work is all."

The grimace became a wicked smile. "Nick got you working already? I thought the new girls got their first week free."

"No. I wasn't working for Nick. I have a job with a beekeeper."

Stella laughed. "Bees? That's rich. We'll see how long that lasts."

The older girl sauntered away, leaving Olivia standing in the entryway. As she closed the door, a cry came from the kitchen. Then Stella shouted, "I need some help in here!"

With a quick jog, Olivia reached the room as Stella helped Molly onto a stool. Molly's sloppy bun was falling apart, red hair spilling over the sides of her face. Olivia came around from behind, and her breath caught in her throat. Molly's left eye was swollen shut, blood dripping from a split lip. "What happened? Did your boyfriend do this to you?"

"Get a towel and some water," Stella ordered.

Olivia ran and got the requested items. By the time she returned, Molly's eye seemed even blacker. "Should I go get Nadine? Or Nick?"

An angry laugh burst out of Stella's mouth. "Wake up, kid. Who do you think hit Molly?"

13

Chapter Thirteen

Olivia froze, her heart thudding at what she'd heard. Sure, she'd seen Nick's controlling side, but violence? It didn't match up to the image in her brain. He'd come across so sweetly when they'd met. She held the towel out to Molly. "Why would Nick hit you?"

Grabbing the towel, Stella pushed Olivia away to stand in front of Molly. Stella dabbed the blood and received a growl in return. "Molly didn't do what Nick wanted tonight. He said she wasn't earning her keep."

Tears mixed with the blood running down Molly's face. She moaned between winces from Stella's clumsy cleaning attempts.

Reality threatened. Olivia couldn't ignore the sinking feeling in her stomach. Afraid to ask, but needing the truth, she gasped out the words she couldn't hold back. "When Emlyn and I were selling Nick's produce... a lot of men were stopping by. I don't think they were there to buy vegetables."

Molly laughed, then grimaced.

"Sorry," Stella said to Molly as she pulled the towel back from her wounded eye. "Our girl here is a real sleuth, huh?" Head cocked, blue eyes piercing, she eyed Olivia. "Honey, the only thing you two sold that day was yourselves."

Numbness crawled down her arms until her fingers tingled. As the realization sank in, she grabbed the island for support, the sharp wooden edge cutting into her fingers. She had to know all of it. "Why is most everyone here new except you two?"

"Girls don't stay for long here. They go out on dates with Nick's friends and don't come back." Slumping back in her chair, Stella set the bloodstained towel on the counter. "We're the lucky ones, aren't we, Molly? We've got steady dates. Or at least we used to."

Molly began sobbing. At first, it was just a moan, but then she couldn't seem to catch her breath as her cries poured into her hands clutching at her face. Stella snugged the other girl into an embrace and rubbed her back in gentle circles.

Feeling like an intruder, Olivia slunk up to her room. When she reached her bed, she flopped onto her back and let her backpack slide to the floor. What was she going to do? It wasn't safe here, but it wasn't safe back at her cousin's house either. At least here she had friends. But if what Stella said was true, none of them would be here for long. They'd all disappear like the girls before them.

She rose to sit on the edge of the bed. Opening her backpack, she unearthed its contents—three apples and two honey jars. She could trade the valuable honey at the market for grits. Of course, she wouldn't have any way to cook grits if she left this house.

Could she survive on her own in the woods? She shivered at the thought of living outside with no protection from snakes, coyotes, or the wild dogs that roamed the woods since the collapse. Perhaps she could find an abandoned home to sleep in. There were plenty around. But then again, so many people had fled the cities. Most of the abandoned buildings were in Columbus or Atlanta, and getting to one of those areas had its risks.

If only her father were still around. When she'd been homeless with him, he'd had her back. Well, at least he had when he'd been sober. Which wasn't often. A tear slipped out. With no good options, she was stuck here, waiting for Nick's next move.

No. That wouldn't do. She needed a plan.

The knock on her door was so quiet, she'd almost missed it. She'd thought she'd imagined it until a louder one followed it. "Come in."

As the door opened, Emlyn peeked in, her wispy hair loose over her shoulders, her eyes red and swollen. "Can I come in?"

"Of course." Olivia patted the mattress beside her. Her stomach twisted. Dare she ask if Nick had done something to Emlyn as well? "You all right?"

Emlyn slid inside and closed the door with a gentle click. She didn't make eye contact as she scooted across the room and plopped into the offered seat. "Have you seen Molly? Her face?"

"Yeah." Olivia nodded. "It's pretty messed up."

Picking up a pillow, Emlyn clutched it to her chest. "I'm afraid."

Her friend looked so miserable with her chin resting on the frilly pink pillow, fingers kneading the fluff. Olivia's gut ached. "Join the club."

The next words came out barely above a whisper. "Nadine

said I don't need to work in the garden tomorrow. There's going to be a party at Nick's place, and I'm supposed to be there—all of us but you are."

A party should be something to look forward to these days. Most people spent every ounce of energy trying to survive. Since grocery stores shut down, getting food on the table was the priority. If Nick wanted the girls at a party instead of working in the garden, that couldn't be good. "Have you ever been to a party at Nick's?"

Emlyn closed her eyes and shook her head. A fresh tear squeezed out. "The other girls are excited. Nadine told them they'd get some pills before the party to relax and get in the mood." A desperate pleading sheened her eyes when she opened them. "I don't want to take drugs. My best friend got addicted to pain pills back before things fell apart. It was awful, watching her life crumble. All she cared about was getting the next high."

Olivia wrapped an arm around her friend and pulled her close. "You don't have to take any drugs. You don't have to go to that party if you don't want to. We can find another way to survive without this place—you and me—together."

Once the words were out, shock shivered over her. Could she keep such a promise? She stiffened her spine, determined to make it true. She was tired of being afraid. Tired of looking for someone else to give her safety and security. Tired of letting life happen to her and ready to make a life on her terms.

"How?" The word came out with a gurgle of phlegm as if Emlyn were drowning in unshed tears. "I don't know how to raise food or hunt or anything else. My mother didn't want me. Chose her crummy boyfriend instead. We can't survive on our own out there."

If only Olivia had a solid plan. If she could give her friend hope for a future that didn't involve Nick or this pink-house prison, then Emlyn would follow her. But she hadn't a clue how to find security for herself, much less someone else. "I'll figure it out. I promise."

A scratching rustled at the door. "Sam." Emlyn sprang off the bed and hustled to the door. "Come on, baby."

As if the cat realized its master needed love, it began purring the minute Emlyn picked it up. Rubbing its head on the girl's neck, the cat stretched and then settled into her arms. "At least Sam loves me."

"Hey, now." Olivia stood and wandered over to pet the animal. "I thought we were friends. I love you too. You're not alone."

When Emlyn made eye contact, a fresh round of tears threatened those gray eyes. "Thank you." She croaked out a soggy response. "I love you too. It's great to have a friend again."

Sleep wouldn't come easily tonight. Thoughts rolled through Olivia's head over and over as if she could find a solution by analyzing the situation from every angle.

What a no-brainer. Going to the party tomorrow would be bad for all the girls, especially for Emlyn. But what could she offer as an alternative? Perhaps Carissa could help them out. After all, she lived on her own and supported herself. The children at the market flocked to her like she was some sort of pied piper. Only, instead of a flute, she had honey candy.

Was it fair to put her problems on the other woman's shoulders? Perhaps if she didn't tell her the sordid details but asked for general advice, she could get ideas without burdening Carissa.

But what could she do about the party tomorrow? Emlyn couldn't go. And what about the rest of her housemates? Could she help them too? She thought of Anna and her love of the library. If she got sucked into taking drugs, the need for them would outweigh any desire to read.

Olivia thrust her legs over the side of the bed and paced from the dresser to the window as thoughts about what her father was like before the collapse chased thoughts of him after Mom died. Even as she grew older, he never stopped being the tickle monster that he'd been when she was little—until he started to drink.

Smiling at the memories, she pressed her forehead to the cool windowpane and relived memories of him chasing her to bed and tickling her until she hid under the covers where the monster couldn't see her. If he tried to stop before she was exhausted, she'd peek back out from under her comforter, and the beast would resume his delightful torment.

Eventually, though, Mom always came in to shoo out the tickle monster and read her a bedtime story. Besides tales of princes who rescued princesses, she also read tales from the Bible. How about the teenager, David, who killed the giant with a stone? If only she were good with a slingshot, she'd protect all the girls in this house from any lecherous men.

She slumped back to the bed, burrowed under the pink comforter, and squeezed her eyes shut.

Sleep came, but not until early morning. She awoke late with the sun shining through her window. Somehow, the fresh day burned away the distressing thoughts.

Time to figure things out.

She got up and dressed, her brain in high gear. Perhaps she could convince the girls not to go to the party tonight.

Breakfast would be her last chance to see them before she left for Carissa's today.

Before heading downstairs, she removed one honey jar from her bag and hid it under the bed. It was valuable, and she'd earned it. She just didn't trust they'd be safe in her room. Too bad she didn't have a way to lock her door.

When she arrived in the kitchen, Emlyn held the cat, cooing as she petted it. She greeted Olivia and pointed toward a pot resting on the stove. "Morning. There's grits this morning—one of those lucky power's-on days."

Anna and Brandy sat at the island, eating. A book rested between them. Anna had one finger holding her place in the book while the other hand worked her spoon. Brandy pushed a chair out and motioned to Olivia. "Stools are a hot commodity this morning. Get the last one while you can."

"Thanks." The dark room, attacked on all sides by brooding wooden cabinets, seemed to suck her into its oppressive void. Olivia moved toward one looming cabinet for a bowl, grabbed a spoon, scooped some grits, and set her breakfast near the proffered seat. After sliding her backpack off, she pulled a honey jar out of her pack. "I brought some honey home last night. You might like it in your grits."

Emlyn's eyes lit up, and she put the cat down to get her breakfast serving. "I can't remember the last time I had honey. You sure you want us to eat it? That's valuable stuff, worth a lot at the market."

Olivia sat in front of her meal and unscrewed the lid from the honey. After dipping her spoon into the golden liquid, she drizzled it across her grits before she passed the jar down.

Just before she brought the first bite to her mouth, she froze in place. Remembering lunch with Carissa, Olivia dipped her spoon back into the bowl. "Would you like to say a prayer with me? Just to thank God for the food?"

Anna shrugged. "I don't know why we would. It's not as if God has been helping us out here."

Brandy took another spoonful of grits and swallowed. "I'm not sure there is a God out there. At least not one interested in listening to me."

Emlyn came over to stand beside Olivia. "I'll pray with you. Mom sent me to Sunday school back when I was little. I think it was just to get me out of the house, 'cause she never went to church. But I used to love praying. It's so peaceful."

Olivia took Emlyn's hand, and they bowed their heads. "Father, thank you for this food and for giving us each other. Please help us take care of each other like you want us to. Amen."

After Emlyn repeated the amen, she eyed Olivia. "I hadn't heard you pray before. Is this something new?"

She stirred her grits, trying to think of the best way to phrase what she wanted to say. "I used to pray with my mom. After she died, Dad didn't pray, and I guess I'd forgotten. But a friend reminded me, and I'd kinda missed it."

They ate their breakfast in companionable silence. Soon, the words just bubbled out. "Don't go to the party tonight. Any of you. Okay?" She reached both hands out to the girls. "We can figure out another way to survive without Nick."

Brandy walked her bowl over to the sink, turned the water on, and rinsed the remnants of breakfast away. "If all I need to do to have my room and board covered is go to some stupid party, then I'm all in. I've been homeless before. It's not fun, and I'm not planning to go back to it."

Olivia shuddered over when she was on the streets with her

dad.

But this wasn't the time to focus on the negative. This was a time for action. "What if I could find another way?"

Anna looked up from her book. "Sweetie, if you can find another way, I'm in."

They all nodded.

Having them all agree was more than she could have hoped for. But now what?

14

Chapter Fourteen

Her steps light, Olivia speed-walked to Carissa's house. There had to be a way to find them all a new home. Someplace safe where they could learn the skills to survive on their own.

She'd been a fool to think she couldn't make it on her own, hadn't she? In her time with her cousin's family, she'd been the one with the ideas. Sure, her aunt and uncle had contributed with sweat equity. She hadn't worked alone. But they hadn't sought new solutions—that was all her doing.

A bunny jumped out of the bushes.

Rabbits!

She'd wanted to talk to Jan about how they raised them for food. It couldn't be that hard. After all, they were teaching Jacob. If a nine-year-old could learn it, so could she.

She needed to set aside the time to trek back to the Worthington farm. No matter what Caleb thought of her family, Jan would help.

In seemingly no time at all, she stood at Carissa's doorstep once again. A quick knock brought the smiling woman to the door. "I guess I should give you a key or something, so you don't have to knock like a visitor."

They'd only worked together one day, and yet Olivia felt as if she were coming home. The offer of the key warmed her inside and made her want to hug the other woman. "I'd love that. Thanks."

"Did you have a good evening? Plenty of sleep?" Carissa led her through the house to the mudroom. "We're picking apples today—going to make applesauce."

As Olivia waited, Carissa tugged on her boots. Then they walked out to a building near the orchard. Carissa opened the shed and handed a long pole with a bag on the end to Olivia. "Have you ever picked apples before?"

A metal ring with toothlike protrusions circled the bag. "Nope, but I'm going to guess we tug them out of the tree with the metal spikes, which will drop them into the bags. Right?"

"Precisely." Carissa emerged from the shed with another pole and two bushel baskets. She gave Olivia one. "There are plenty of bees out there, enjoying the apples that have gotten too ripe and are leaking juice. Glad we know you're not allergic, but still, be careful when you unload your bag."

"Got it."

They walked up to the first tree in the straight orchard rows. Yellow orbs bowed the overloaded branches. Carissa dropped her basket and extended her pole to a grouping of apples. "You don't want to bruise the fruit."

She slid the metal teeth down the branch while lifting the bag upward. After stripping the apples from the end of the branch, she walked her hands up the pole until the heavily laden bag reached her hands. Then she upended the container into the basket. "See? Easy-peasy."

It looked simple enough.

Olivia stepped up to the same tree. She repeated the maneuver she'd witnessed and came away with a similar bounty. "This is easy."

Carissa's huge grin and twinkling eyes hinted there was a factor she hadn't considered. "It is… at first. We'll talk again in an hour."

An hour? Olivia rolled her eyes. She could put in more time than that. No wimp here.

Lifting her pole again, she set to work as Carissa glided to the tree's opposite side.

Soon, she'd filled her basket halfway with beautiful apples. The heavenly scent tickled her nose, but she realized why Carissa had set the hour limit. After they gathered the low-hanging fruit, she had to reach higher and higher into the leaves and branches to capture all the orbs. Her shoulder muscles burned, and her neck felt like it was on fire from the repetitive movements.

Once they filled the baskets, Carissa brought out more. By the end of the hour, four containers overflowed with fruit, and Olivia's arms ached to stay below her shoulders.

She picked an apple off the ground that had toppled off the pile. "I don't mean to be a quitter, but I don't think I could lift this pole one more time. I'm exhausted."

Carissa laughed. "Seems simple until you try doing it for a while. We've got enough here to keep us busy the rest of today with processing." She came to stand beside Olivia's basket. "Grab the other handle. We'll carry this one in first."

Together, they carted all the apples into the kitchen. After the last basket rested on the white-tile floor, their golden-yellow color complementing the sunny kitchen, Carissa pulled two glasses out of the cabinet, filled them with water, and handed Olivia one. "Next, we need to peel the apples and slice them into a pot. I've got an outdoor fire pit and, believe it or not, my grandmother's cast iron cooking kettle. It's the old-fashioned way to go, but since we never know when the power will be on or off, it ensures the applesauce gets finished once we start."

The excitement of learning a new skill kept Olivia's attention riveted. Since she'd helped the Worthingtons can beans, the process wasn't foreign to her, but she'd never made applesauce. If only they had cinnamon, her favorite seasoning with apples. But she doubted that spice existed anywhere in Georgia by now. "Do you want me to peel or slice?"

Carissa opened a drawer and slid out a vegetable peeler. "I like how you think. Tell you what, you peel, and I'll get the fire started."

Olivia had a good-sized stack ready for slicing by the time Carissa came back inside, smelling of smoke. "Fire's ready, and the pot's just waiting to be filled."

Olivia pointed the peeler at the pile of apples. "Want me to switch to slicing so you can get some over the fire sooner?"

"Sure." Carissa eyed the heap. "Let's do this first pot together. Then we can split the jobs again."

As they worked side by side, Olivia couldn't keep her thoughts to herself any longer. Unsure how to broach the subject, she just blurted out, "I've got a problem."

Carissa kept working. "I can't guarantee a solution, but I'm happy to talk through things. Whatcha got?"

How to be discreet, and yet still get the critical points across?

"I've got a friend who might be getting in too deep with the wrong guy, but she feels like she doesn't have any other options." Part of her wanted to see her employer's reaction, but the rest of her wanted to be certain it came across as a casual conversation. She probably couldn't keep her eyes from betraying her. "It's not as if there are plenty of jobs these days or other ways to take care of yourself. I wish I knew how you got all of this on your own."

She waved her hand in the air to encompass the house and farm in the *all* she meant.

Carissa continued to slice. "Believe it or not, I fell into that trap myself when I was younger."

Whoa. Olivia stopped her knife movements and gawked. "Really?"

"Don't look so surprised. It happens all the time. I don't think we're born with it, but somewhere along the line, some of us buy into the belief that we want a man to rescue the damsel in distress." She huffed out a laugh. "Though the number of those who are their own heroes grows by the day."

"Is that how you got this place? Did a guy buy it for you?"

Carissa raised an eyebrow again. "I wish. No, I take that back. I'm glad I worked for this on my own." She scraped the slices of fresh apple off her cutting board and into a glass mixing bowl, the core and seeds into a separate bucket. "Because of a relationship that went sideways, I ended up here."

There was a story here. Eager to hear more, Olivia waved her hand to prompt Carissa. "Go on."

"I married young—too young, it turned out. My husband was going to save me from all my troubles." She blew out a deep breath. "Whoo-eee. That didn't work out."

Since they'd almost finished slicing, Olivia returned to her peeler, selected an apple, and relieved it of its skin. "Did you end up divorced?"

"No. I'm still married—I think."

"You *think* you're still married? Don't you know?"

"If you don't have a clue whether your spouse is still alive, then you can't exactly know whether you're still married." Carissa divvied the slices and the cores once more into their various containers. "My husband wanted to control me—where to work, what to wear, who to associate with—the whole shebang. It was subtle at first. I probably wouldn't have married him if he'd started out that way."

"What was he like?"

A sad smile twisted Carissa's lips as she described her husband. "He was sweet and attentive. That's what attracted me. He complimented my intelligence, my looks, and anything else." Her hands slowed on the apples, her eyes glazing. "I'd been ignored by my parents. I think they hadn't planned on me and didn't know what to do with a kid. I spent a lot of time alone. When Diego came along, he gave me all the attention I thought I needed. It was hard to resist someone who pours all that affection on you—especially when you're starved to be seen."

Olivia understood. She'd gone unnoticed, as if she were invisible, ever since her mother died. Dad seemed lost and clueless about how to raise his daughter alone. He hadn't seemed capable of living without Mom himself. "I know how that feels."

Olivia's words jerked Carissa back to the present. "Sorry. Back to the reason he's gone. In his family, the men were dominant and the women subservient. I bought into that, but then realized I was losing my identity. I fell into a deep depression."

"Did you have friends to help you out?"

"No. He didn't like me going out with my girlfriends, so in

time, it was just me and him." She accepted a peeled apple from Olivia and began slicing it. "I needed a counselor, a professional to talk to, and I couldn't afford one. But a local church offered a free service to its members. I joined the church and got some therapy."

Olivia had never thought of a church as a counseling resource. "Did the counselor try to convert you?"

"Nope. But the pastor's sermons did the trick. He was an amazing speaker. I would have sworn the Holy Spirit stood behind him on that pulpit every Sunday—powerful and moving lessons, every week. He showed how Jesus treated women in the Bible. They weren't property to him. They were valuable people in their own right. That made me realize I wasn't owned by my husband, and I insisted we get counseling together to figure out our marriage."

"Did it get better then?"

Carissa's gleaming brown eyes dimmed. "No. He didn't want an independent woman. Instead, he moved in with my former best friend. He didn't want *me* to spend time with her, but *he* didn't keep himself away. Funny how it worked out that way."

How betrayed Carissa must have felt. Olivia's stomach fell. "I'm sorry."

"It was all for the best." With the back of a sticky hand, Carissa swiped a wisp of hair away from her face. "That was right before the variant struck. I couldn't afford the enormous house after he left, and he didn't intend to support two women. So, I found this little slice of heaven." She twirled her knife in the air. "And just in time too. Who knew what a blessing this place would be in a few short years?"

Blessing indeed. If only Olivia had her own place. "It's beautiful here."

"I got off topic there, didn't I? Let's talk about this friend of yours. She needs to find a way to support herself, and she needs a safe place to stay. Does she have relatives she could turn to? Family is the first resource for everyone."

What about her family? If she'd told her aunt and uncle what Rob had done, would they have taken care of her instead of protecting him? She hadn't even given them a chance. They were family, after all. "She might. I'll suggest that to her."

"Excellent." Carissa slid her latest batch of slices into the almost overflowing bowl. "Let's get these apples into that kettle. Still lots to do today."

«»

Olivia felt rich as she walked up the sidewalk to the pink house. They'd canned dozens of jars of applesauce, and her payment was six of them. Apples filled the remaining room in her pack. The weight on her back comforted and exhilarated her.

Once again, she found the door locked when she tried to turn the knob. She knocked—and waited. Knocked again. Nothing. Why hadn't she gotten a key yet? She must ask for one as soon as she found someone to let her in.

Oh. Right. Nick's party was tonight.

She trudged across the street. As she approached the house, music and laughing drifted from out back beyond the pool's privacy fence. Lifting the gate latch, she peeked in, then slammed her eyelids shut. If only she could unsee what she'd seen.

Her friends from the pink house were all there, along with several older men. Some men she recognized from her day at the vegetable stand. All the girls wore skimpy bathing suits.

Her stomach turned when she spotted Emlyn—topless. A

man groped her as they swayed to the music. She wobbled on her feet as if she were drunk—or drugged. All the girls were in similar straits.

Stepping back, Olivia closed the gate and hurried across the street. She'd sleep outside if she had to, but no way she was going into that backyard. That wasn't her kind of party.

15

Chapter Fifteen

There had to be a way back into the pink house without asking for a key tonight. And, if there was, Olivia would find it. Just for the sake of thoroughness, she jiggled the knob on the front door once more to verify its status. Definitely locked. *Rats*.

She went around to the back door and tested it as well. No luck.

This wasn't over yet. There had to be a way.

Her day with Carissa crept into her mind. The woman's faith was strong—like Mom's. If Mom were here now, Olivia knew what would already have happened.

Bowing her head, she closed her eyes. "Father, I know it's been a while. Too long, I know. I don't want to be like my friends and give in to what Nick wants. Please help me find a way in. I could use guidance to help them too, because I know you love all of us, no matter what. Amen."

Her mission was obvious—get inside and hope her friends came home soon. She began a trek around the perimeter and checked the first-floor windows one at a time. Someone might have locked them, or maybe they'd been painted shut. After years of color changes and fresh coats, so much paint could have sealed them. If so, it would be hopeless to try.

Then she saw it. An open window. Probably the office window, though she'd lost track in the dark. It was just a tad too high for her. She went back to the old shed behind the house in search of something to stand on. She flipped over a sturdy bucket, dumped out the rags in it, and stepped onto it. It held.

Carrying it back to the window, she used it to climb up and shimmy in through the opening. With the desk in front of the window, she got down on the other side easily.

As she walked through toward her bedroom, she couldn't escape the scene from Nick's house. Emlyn's drugged look terrified her. If only she could've grabbed Emlyn and stolen her away from the party.

Lying on her bed, she crossed her hands behind her head and peered at the tree shadows dancing across the ceiling, seemingly keeping time with the music across the street. A shiver coursed over her, and she flopped onto her stomach. She had to prove to Emlyn and the other girls they could survive without Nick's help.

Right. Help. As if that's what he was doing. The only one he was helping was himself, and these girls were commodities, like sweet fruit from the produce stand.

Concentrate, Olivia.

If it weren't for Rob, she could go back to her family and take Emlyn with her. But why should she allow him to rule her life? Her uncle promised her father—they were going to take care of her. They couldn't address Rob's behavior if they didn't know.

Tomorrow, she'd head back. She'd set things straight and give her uncle a chance to live up to his promise.

«»

Dawn couldn't come soon enough. She'd drifted in and out of sleep all night, waiting to hear her friends returning. They never did. At least she hadn't heard them. Now that the sun's first rays broke over the horizon, it was time for action.

She sat up in bed. Maybe they came home after she'd drifted off. Needing to check on Emlyn, she sprang out of bed. As she grabbed her jeans off the floor, her heart raced. What if Emlyn hadn't come home? Then what? Would it do any good to confront Nick and demand to know where her friend was? Unlikely.

Pants on, she jogged to Emlyn's room. With a gentle knock on the bedroom door, she wasn't sure whether to whisper. It was early, and if she'd come home last night, it would have been late. Or perhaps very early this morning. There was no response from inside.

Forget caution. She needed to know. She knocked again, louder this time. "Emlyn?"

Still no response.

She opened the door and peeked inside. The bed was empty—no Emlyn.

Her heart stuttered for a second. A shiver shot down her spine. What if she was too late to save her friends?

She jogged down to the second floor and knocked on the first door she came to. There was no response. She looked inside—empty.

Was she the only person in the house now?

Frantic to find anyone else at home, she ran to the next room, shouting as she banged on the door. "Hello? Is anyone else home?"

A voice made her jump.

"Will you stop already? How's anyone supposed to sleep with you making all that racket? It's like the crack of dawn. Shut up already."

Stella leaned on her doorframe with the door opened wide enough to show her exhausted face. "Please, can we sleep in peace?"

Relief wobbled Olivia's knees. At least one girl in the house was home. "Where's everyone else? Did Emlyn come home last night?"

"Do I look like I could be her mama? It's not my job to keep tabs on every girl who comes through this house. Go away."

Stella retreated to her room with a less-than-gentle closing of the door.

Nice. How's that for looking out for friends?

Obviously, Olivia couldn't count on anyone else to help.

She went downstairs and found the front door partly open. Shivers crawled over her skin. She shut it and twisted the deadbolt. Had Stella left it that way when she'd come in?

A low moan came from the living room. Olivia sprinted in that direction. Emlyn, Anna, and Brandy lined up and slumped over each other on the couch. It looked as though they'd dragged themselves into the house and passed out together.

Breath rushed out of Olivia's mouth, and every muscle loosened with its escaping whoosh.

Anna was at the far end with the built-in recliner's foot extension pushed out. Brandy's head rested in her lap as she lay curled in a ball, feet tucked up close. Emlyn's feet rested on Brandy's hip. Her head lolled on the couch's opposite end. With a moaning grumble, Brandy attempted to push Emlyn's feet off.

At least Olivia knew where these three were. Molly was probably alive and with Stella in their shared room. But what about Lilly or Ruby?

Olivia did a thorough search of the rest of the house, including the library turret, but she didn't see them. Not sure what else to do, she went back to her room and opened her backpack. She took all but two of the jars out and hid them with the others.

She also left two apples with the jars. Best to be sure she had food available should she get shut off again. Somehow, she doubted she and Nick would ultimately agree on her new job. Or on the correct payment for rent.

But then again, perhaps today would go better than she hoped.

Returning downstairs, she left apples for each of the girls on the counter. They'd wake up, and they'd be hungry. She got a paper and pen out of the office and left a note with the fruit. "Apples from my job for everyone to share. See you tonight. Love, Olivia."

With one last peek at her sleeping roommates, she headed out the back door. Today would be a hike, but she'd make it back to her family and have a much-needed conversation.

By the time she reached the house, she had only one apple left, and the sun had almost risen to its midday arch. As she walked up, just five of the dozen chickens pecked around in the yard. She stilled, eyeing them and wondering where the rest of the flock had gone.

The wooden steps leading to the front door creaked as she walked across them. Knocking on the door felt strange, but just walking in felt odd as well. When no one responded, she tried a few more times, but they mustn't be home.

They always left a key under the welcome mat. She lifted the edge, prepared to let herself in to wait, but the key was peeking out of a piece of folded paper. Picking it up, she opened the paper and read. "Olivia, if you find this, we're not home, but come on in the house. Detailed note on the table."

Strange.

She unlocked and opened the door. Power was out in the house, and the lack of any sound made her hold her breath and listen. No ticking clocks, no rustling curtains, no murmuring voices.

On the kitchen table, they'd propped an envelope up between the empty salt and pepper shakers. Someone had scrawled one word on it—*Olivia*.

Her hands shaking, she picked it up and slid her finger underneath the flap to break the seal. She wasn't sure she wanted to know what they had to say. Her heart didn't have room for one more ounce of rejection.

Deal with it.

Unfolding the paper, she read the moment her eyes could focus on the first sentence.

Olivia,

We're sorry. You just can't know how sorry we are. Your dad left you here so we could take care of you, and we meant to. But we got too wrapped up in Rob's disease to focus on what was happening right in front of us.

Rob confessed what he did to you, and it opened all our eyes to what needed to happen. If you find this note and an empty home, then we're still on a new journey of healing for our family. We're taking Rob to Atlanta to find a doctor who can help him stop drinking. It's not the safest trip in the world, so we can't guarantee we'll make it back. But we also can't keep on keeping on as if things are all right in our home.

Please, stay here if you like. If we don't return, this is your home now. We know it isn't much, but if anyone can turn it into something habitable, you can.

You've been the one with all the ideas for keeping food on our table. There just aren't enough words to thank you for that. If we make it back, we'll all do our best to make it up to you.

Until we see you again, please know we love you and we're so proud of you and all you've accomplished so far.

Hugs,

Aunt Amanda, Uncle Kevin, and Rob

A tear fell on the word *proud*, smudging the last sentence. That same feeling surged through her chest. If only they were here now. She wanted to wrap each of them in her arms and squeeze them until they cried uncle. Even her crazy cousin Rob.

She'd not been close to them before she moved in, so she hadn't really known Rob as a sober person. What would he be like if he wasn't drunk?

Her father had been loving before he started imbibing too much. The best memories of him involved tickle fights, bike rides on the river walk, and camping trips. He taught her the joys of the campout, the tricks to build a fire and make a s'more. She could almost smell the smoky marshmallow and taste the sweet, gooey chocolate and graham cracker.

She'd give anything for one more camping trip with her parents.

Enough.

She had things to figure out. She had a home again. That

was a tremendous advantage. She didn't need to go back to the pink house. But if she was going to convince Emlyn or any of the other girls to leave the pink house, she'd have to prove to them they could take care of themselves.

They had everything they needed to cut trees into firewood. There should still be several felled trees in the woods Uncle Kevin and Rob downed so they could begin the drying-out process. The saw required two people to work, but she knew how to use it and could teach the others.

With five chickens left, she still had eggs. She understood now. They must've left the shed open so the chickens could get out to forage. Unfortunately, that left them unprotected at night from raccoons, coyotes, and other nocturnal predators. Tonight, she'd be sure to lock them in.

A quick peek at the pantry told her what she'd suspected. Not a crumb to be found. Of course, they'd had to take any food with them. Though they likely hadn't had much to take.

She opened her backpack, pulled out two jars of applesauce, and set them on the pantry shelves.

Not much, but it was a start—her own food stock. That pantry would be full someday. If everything went as she hoped, she'd need a lot more to feed all the girls from the pink house. That is… if she could convince them to leave Nick.

Nick. Just thinking his name made the hairs on the back of her neck stand up, and a knot formed in her stomach. She saw him for what he was now. He used young girls. Treated them like assets the same as you'd treat a home or a car.

She was going to do everything in her power to put an end to him owning any girl in the future, and she was starting with her friends in the pink house. This place would be their refuge, and she would make sure it could sustain all of them.

Your time for reckoning is coming, Nicholas Davis. And when it came, she hoped he fell hard—hard enough to see stars.

16

Chapter Sixteen

Olivia slid the key back under the mat. The rest of the day promised miles' worth of walking, so she'd borrowed a pair of her uncle's thick alpaca socks he kept in reserve. Coupled with her threadbare ones, the extra cushioning would keep her feet from blistering.

Sore feet or not, her mission remained. By the time she made it to Carissa's house, she devoured the apples she'd brought for breakfast. Knowing Carissa expected her, she rapped once on the door and let herself in with a bellowed greeting. "Morning, sunshine!"

Carissa met her as she entered the kitchen, her normal grin warm and welcoming. "You seem chipper today. Ready to pick apples?"

Olivia dropped her backpack on the counter. "Whatever. I do have a favor to ask, though."

Carissa raised an eyebrow. "Of course. Whatcha need?"

Butterflies fluttered in her stomach. "I moved back to my family's home, and I want to raise bees there. Teach me how to start?"

With a clap, Carissa danced a little jig. "I was hoping you'd want to try it yourself. Wasn't sure you felt confident enough to face a hive on your own, though." She gave Olivia's shoulder a playful jab. "Good for you."

The butterflies fled, taking the tension cocooning her muscles with them. "I hoped you'd say that. Truthfully, I'm still a wee bit terrified, but I'm going to get past it."

"I've got just the thing to get you started. I haven't used it in a while, but it'll be perfect for you to begin. Follow me."

They marched out to the shed. Carissa used a ladder to pull a purple painted wooden box out of the rafters and lowered it to Olivia. "Grab this."

Eyebolts attached to the top as if it would hang on something. A narrow slit opened the front on the opposite end of the hardware.

"Obviously, the opening is for bees to go in and out, but it's sealed other than that. How do we use it?"

Carissa descended, then clattered open a toolbox drawer. She selected two hooks from her various bits of hardware and brought them over to Olivia, demonstrating how they would hook through the eyebolts. "We drill these hooks into a tree, then attach the box with the bolts. Ta-da—catch box."

"Catch box?"

"Let me show you."

Back at the toolbox, Carissa got out a screwdriver and removed the hardware holding the top of the catch box on. She then picked up some frames they'd recently extracted the honey from with only the empty comb remaining. She swooshed her long hair aside as she slid the frames into the box. "We don't have any more time this year. So, I'll split one of my hives into two and bring you one of those. But next year, you'll be ready to catch one of the first swarms. We'll give them some used comb to clean up and use as a base."

Olivia paid close attention to the way Carissa slid the frames in and resealed the box. "What makes bees want to settle in the box? Do they like purple or something?"

Tapping on the sealed container, Carissa pulled a vial from the workbench drawer. "We're going to set this box on your property and bait it with some lemongrass oil."

"Then what? This doesn't look like one of your hive boxes."

"No, this one is only for catching a swarm. We'll hang it high in a tree. Once you've caught a swarm, we'll transfer them into a regular hive."

Olivia contemplated the trek back to her uncle's home while carrying the box. The price of the materials alone might put the project out of her reach for a while. "What will I owe you for the hive and this box? Or can I borrow it?"

Hands on her hips, Carissa shook her head. "On market day, I can pick you up to help with the table. I'll drop off the equipment to get started then. You can borrow what you need. I have plenty. That'll get you up and running. Teamwork, right?"

Heat prickled the backs of her eyes as Olivia went weak at the knees. What would she have done without this woman in her life?

She held her hand out. "Thank you. I can't wait. And you won't regret having me work for you at the market. I'm a great runner. Your honey will fly off the table once I reconnect with my regulars."

With a nod and a tap on the box, Carissa pointed to the orchard. "Let's get going, then. Lots more canning to do."

Olivia tried to refuse payment after the workday. It would

weigh her down too much when she picked up her jars from the pink house. Carissa insisted she'd hold on to Olivia's share of the canning and drop it off along with the beekeeping supplies.

Later, as she walked toward town, thoughts of her friends swirled in her brain. Emlyn would move in with her. She was sure of it. Maybe some of the other girls would as well. If her family came back, she'd find a way to make them all fit. She'd solve that problem another day, though. Today, she only needed to convince Emlyn.

By the time she arrived at the pink house, the sun had slipped over the horizon. Whew, the front door was unlocked. Once inside, she did a quick check of the common areas downstairs but didn't find anyone.

She jogged up the stairs to collect the jars from her room. Good. They were where she'd left them. After she'd gathered her belongings, the pack and overloaded pillowcase weighed on her.

The silence in the house felt eerie—as if something were wrong. She dropped her pack at her door, then knocked on her friend's door. "Emlyn, it's me, Olivia. You in there?"

No response. She knocked again but still heard nothing. So she opened the door and let herself in. A figure lay on the bed, curled up in a ball with the covers over her head. "Emlyn? You awake?"

Some snuffling sound came, then a quiet mumble. "Go away."

Olivia advanced toward the bed and sat on the edge. She tugged back the covers to check on her friend, but Emlyn faced the wall. When Emlyn yanked at the covers, trying to pull them back over her head, Olivia wouldn't allow it. "Come on. I need to talk to you. I've got some exciting news."

"Ugh." Emlyn moaned, flopped over, and squinted at Olivia

through a tangle of gossamer hair. After squeezing her eyes shut again, she palmed the pale strands away from her face. "I'm tired. Can't we talk later?"

Was Emlyn awake enough to understand? "No. Now. This is important."

With a grumble, Emlyn allowed Olivia to pull the comforter down. She then sat up beside her. Slumping onto the knees she drew up to her chest, she pressed her face into them. "Ph–f–fine."

"You aren't going to believe it. My cousin's family went to Atlanta and left me the house to use. I've already got a pantry started." She patted her backpack as the wonderful words burst out, rapid fire. "And I've got chickens. We're going to cut wood to sell, raise bees, and learn about rabbits too. This is something we can do. We don't have to stay here and do Nick's bidding."

No excitement animated Emlyn's face as she tipped it away from her knees. She scrunched her nose. "What are you talking about? I don't know how to do any of those things."

"No, *you* don't, but *I* do. I'll teach you, and we can manage it together." Olivia wrapped her arm around Emlyn's shoulders, jostling her like a little sister. "You don't have to live here and work for Nick. None of us do. We can be free to work for ourselves."

"But what if it doesn't work? You said yourself living in your family's home wasn't safe. What if they come back and we have to leave? Then what?" Emlyn pulled away. "No. I'll stay here. I've got a bed to sleep in and three meals a day. It's safer here."

Something heavy pressed on Olivia's body. How could Emlyn believe the pink house meant safety? "Didn't you see

Molly's face? You didn't look all that happy when you were running around half naked at Nick's pool the other day."

Emlyn flushed crimson, and she hid behind her hands. Her words came out muffled from behind her palms. "Leave me alone. You don't understand. Nick just wants to take care of us, but we have to help and do our part."

It took a tremendous effort to peel Emlyn's fingers away from her face so Olivia could make eye contact. When she connected, Emlyn's eyes had reddened to match her face, and the pooled tears began their descent.

Olivia took a slow deep breath in, then released it as she held Emlyn's trembling hands. "No. You don't have to help Nick. Worry about yourself before you end up addicted to those drugs he's pushing—or beat up like Molly—or maybe even gone like the girls before us." She took in the pain on her friend's face and soothed with her voice. "Let no man enslave you."

Emlyn's body convulsed. It felt as if her friend's sadness had no end, but after a few minutes, she quieted and wiped her eyes on her T-shirt.

Olivia tugged a shirt out of her backpack and handed it over. "Here. You can snot all over this one. I'll wash it later."

Emlyn half-laughed and half-sobbed as she accepted the clothing and blew her nose into the material.

"Do you think it'll work?" The pleading in her eyes made her look like a twelve-year-old who'd lost her best friend. "Can we leave here and survive?"

"Sweetie." Olivia's heart ached for her bestie to understand. "You aren't safe here. There's no comparison to how much better you'll be there. No matter what."

The lowering of Emlyn's head eventually turned into a

raising of it, which morphed into a couple of nods. "Yes. Okay. Let's do it. But we need to leave now before it's too late. I'm supposed to be at another party tonight. The other girls already left. Nick will look for me soon if I don't show up."

Olivia twisted her lips to one side at the disappointing news. She'd have no chance to invite the other girls to join them tonight. But at least she had Emlyn. "Let's go then."

They had the essentials packed up and ready to go faster than Olivia had thought possible. As they headed down the stairs, the front door opened.

"Emlyn, come on." Ruby's childlike voice carried through the house. "Nick said to get your butt moving. Company is already arriving. Where are you?"

Olivia froze in place, one hand gripping Emlyn's, the other on the banister. Should they tell Ruby what they were doing and ask her to come with them? Or should they avoid her and let them all find out later?

Emlyn had her hand clamped over her mouth, eyes wide and head shaking. That settled Olivia's decision. She put a finger to her lips.

Ruby's steps shuffled through the house. Then she started up the stairway, all the time calling for Emlyn. "Come on. You're going to get us both in trouble. Nick's waiting."

Olivia grasped Emlyn's hand and led her back up the stairs and to Olivia's bedroom. Once there, she pushed Emlyn into the closet, then joined her, closing them in.

As they waited, Ruby stomped into Emlyn's room, then back out of it and down the hall to Olivia's room. "Emlyn? You in here?"

Olivia's heart pounded in her chest.

Oh please, Lord. Don't let her look in the closet.

Then Ruby made a hasty and noisy descent back down the stairway. Relief whooshed out as Olivia released the breath she'd been holding.

Grabbing Emlyn's hand, she whispered. "Let's go. Before she comes back."

They moved, quick and quiet as they could down the hallway. The moment the front door clicked closed, they headed down the stairs. On the first floor, Olivia steered them through the dark-paneled hall, seemingly darker today, to the back of the house—no sense risking someone else coming through to search for Emlyn.

As she turned the knob to leave, the front door opened. Nick called out, "Emlyn. Where are you?"

Olivia's heart leaped into her throat, pounding and choking her with every beat. Emlyn clamped onto her arm, and her eyes grew wide with panic. Once more, Olivia placed her finger over her lips.

His rapid steps clomped into the kitchen. "You'd better get down here. People are waiting."

She lifted a silent prayer. *Help us, please.*

If they didn't get out the door soon, he'd find them on a walk through. She had to risk the door making noise.

They stepped back as she opened the door. Then she pushed Emlyn out and followed. Once outside, she pulled the door after her but didn't risk making sounds by closing it.

Turning to Emlyn, she winced at the terror in her eyes. She clamped her free hand on the other girl's wrist and yanked her away. "Let's go."

17

Chapter Seventeen

Olivia felt like the richest person in the world when she awoke the next morning. She was back in her old bedroom with the sun streaming in through the curtains. A new day filled with opportunity awaited. Sitting up in bed, she arched her back, stretching catlike, then wiggled for the joy of movement.

It was like starting a whole new life, and she wasn't alone. Come to think of it, she'd better check on her friend who'd camped out in Rob's bedroom.

She padded down the hallway and knocked on her cousin's door. "Morning. You up?"

No response.

The door wasn't fully closed, so she gave it a gentle push and peeked inside.

Empty. Emlyn must already be up and looking for breakfast.

After a peek in the bathroom, she went to the kitchen. Also empty.

Huh. Her heartbeat skittered. Was it possible that Emlyn had returned to Nick in the middle of the night?

"Emlyn?"

She jogged through the house, looking in each room. Soon, she stood on the front porch. Then she remembered their conversation on the walk home last night. Emlyn'd been fascinated by the idea of chickens and the excitement of raising baby chicks.

Olivia bounded down the front steps and jogged to the shed. Sure enough, the chickens were pecking around for bugs. Someone had let them out this morning. "Emlyn?"

"In here." The muffled words emanated from inside the shed. "You aren't going to believe this."

When she stepped through the door, Emlyn had piled dozens of eggs into a bucket and was searching for more. Relief that her friend was still here flooded Olivia. "You're up early."

Emlyn set the bucket down gingerly, eyes beaming and smile glorious. "I couldn't wait to look for eggs like you were talking about last night. I didn't know chickens would lay this many. We've got enough to sell at the market."

Olivia knew the truth. She'd not checked on the eggs since her return, and the chickens only laid one egg per day. With the dozen birds they'd started with and five chickens still laying, that meant the bucket held days' worth of eggs.

"I hate to break it to you, but we can't sell or eat those eggs."

Emlyn's eyes grew wide, and her lips turned down. "But why?"

"We don't know how old they are, and we don't know how long they're good for. They might have left right after I did. We can't risk eating or selling a bad egg."

"But there must be a way to tell if the eggs are bad. Maybe we should just crack some open to see?"

Her friend made sense. There had to be a way to figure it

out. "Tell you what. Let's gather them up and put them in the house. On market day, we'll find someone who's selling eggs and ask them how to know. Deal?"

The grin returned, even brighter than before. "Deal."

After a thorough search of the shed, they brought their bounty back to the house and set the egg bucket in the kitchen. "Whatever eggs are there tomorrow morning, we'll have for breakfast, but today, we're having applesauce. Then we need to cut firewood."

Emlyn moved to the sink and washed her hands. "This is so exciting, yet terrifying at the same time. I can't believe we're trying this on our own."

"I know." Olivia pulled the applesauce out of the pantry and set it on the table. "I hope we can convince the other girls to join us. I don't want anyone to live in the pink house."

The mention of their former home lay like a wet blanket over their mealtime. All she could think of was Stella cleaning up Molly's bloodied face, Anna reading to Brandy, and the fear she'd felt when they found Ruby and Lilly passed out. She had to convince them all to leave Nick.

They were ready for their first official task as independent women. "Let's get out in the woods and get some firewood to sell at the market tomorrow."

She hunted down the heavier shoes her aunt had worn while working. Thankfully, she hadn't taken them with her. Though they were too large for Emlyn, two sets of her uncle's woolen socks filled the extra space. A hat from Rob's room and her aunt's gloves completed Emlyn's outfit.

They were ready to work.

Each of them grabbed one handle of the two-man saw while Olivia lugged a maul in her other hand and Emlyn carried the wedge. With the tools weighing them down, they had to take several breaks on the walk to the fallen trees.

"First things first." Olivia nodded to the oak log when they arrived at the first fallen tree. "We need to slice this into sixteen-inch sections before we split each section into firewood."

She pointed to a line she'd scratched into the saw's metal blade with a screwdriver when she'd worked with her aunt. "We'll measure our cuts with the saw—from the tip of the handle to this mark."

"Got it." Emlyn assessed where to set the saw down.

Pushing and pulling the teeth of the two-man saw through the log was hard work—too hard for them to chatter, but that gave them both plenty of time to think.

They'd only gotten two sections done, then had to take a break to catch their breath.

"I'm not sure I'm cut out for this kind of thing." Emlyn swigged some water. "My arms feel like rubber already."

Olivia sipped from her own thermos. "You'll get used to it. You just have to build up muscle."

Emlyn twisted the lid onto her thermos and slid it into her backpack. "Are you sure we can take care of ourselves? I'm already starving. This is a lot of work after just applesauce for breakfast, and we can't even eat those eggs. What are we going to have for supper?"

Olivia's thoughts had been along these same lines as her stomach rumbled too. "Tomorrow is market day. I've got honey to trade, and Carissa will bring the rest of my share of the applesauce we made together. I'll teach you how to run trades and maybe Carissa will let both of us work for her until we can get enough wood cut to set up our sales business."

Emlyn put her hand over her belly. "And for supper tonight?"

"Hopefully, we'll have fresh eggs in the nest when we get home. Then we'll have good protein to go with the applesauce." She placed her thermos in her backpack. "Also, Carissa is bringing us a hive to set up. Next year, we'll have our *own* honey to sell. We can do this."

Emlyn looked at her sideways, twisting her mouth before she spoke. "I hope so. We took a risk leaving the pink house. I can't imagine Nick will let us come back if this doesn't work out."

Heat flared in Olivia's brain. If thoughts were paper, flames would shoot out of her ears as she spoke. "We're never going back there—either of us—no matter what."

Putting her palms forward, Emlyn backed away. "All right already. Calm down." She pointed at the log sections. "What's next?"

Tamping down her frustration, Olivia focused on the task. "We need to split it into logs. Help me put this piece on the tree stump."

They walked over to the section closest to the tree stump and used every bit of remaining strength to lift the log into place.

"Your face is practically purple," Emlyn said. "Maybe I should do the next part. Just tell me what to do."

Picking up the wedge and the maul, Olivia handed Emlyn the maul and balanced the wedge point side down in the center of the wood slice. "The hardest part is getting started. You need to tap the top of the wedge into the wood with the maul. I'll hold the wedge while you give it a tap. Okay?"

Eyebrows raised, Emlyn stepped back. "You sure about that? What if I miss?"

"Don't."

With a shrug, Emlyn lifted the maul into the air, arms shaky, and let it fall.

It hit the wedge hard and ricocheted, slamming Olivia on the cheek.

"Argh!" she screamed out as she clamped her hands over her face.

Hot tears washed over her throbbing cheek and hands.

Emlyn hopped up and down, hands fluttering in the air. "I'm so sorry. What can I do? How can I help?" She tried to pull Olivia's hands away from her face. "Let me see. Oh, how bad is it?"

Olivia backed away, wrenching the groping hands away from her face. "Don't help!"

They danced around for a minute, Emlyn trying to inspect the damage and Olivia trying to escape the assistance.

Finally, though her face still throbbed, the shock had worn off enough for Olivia to allow Emlyn to peel her hands back to see how bad her face looked.

"Ooh, I'm so sorry," Emlyn crooned. "Your eye is already turning colors along with your cheek. It looks awfully puffy. We'd better get you back home before your eye swells shut."

Getting back to the house took twice as long as her eye continued to swell, making the path harder to see. The entire way back, Emlyn apologized over and over while Olivia tried to assure her it was an understandable accident.

Back in the kitchen, Olivia sat while Emlyn soaked a dish towel and helped her place it over the inflamed cheek and eye.

"Accidents happen." She'd already said the words a hundred times. "We'll know next time to find a safer way to get the wedge set."

"I should have known to be more careful."

She couldn't handle watching Emlyn pace between the sink and the table. Perhaps if she distracted her with a task, she'd calm down. "Why don't we get supper ready?"

Emlyn froze in place as if the idea had stunned her. "I can do that. What are we having? More applesauce?"

"Let's go get today's eggs and have those. I'll show you where the chives grow, and you can add those in."

With furrowed eyebrows, Emlyn brought a fresh, dampened towel for Olivia's eye. "What's a chive?"

How could she not know what a chive was?

"It's a plant, kind of like a green onion or a shallot, but the bulb at the end is very tiny. You chop it up and add it to the eggs for flavor."

"I'll go get the eggs. You should probably rest here."

The way her head was throbbing, she couldn't agree more. "Thanks."

As the door shut behind Emlyn, Olivia went to the bathroom to see the damage done to her face. She winced. The night Nick hit her, Molly looked better than the person who stared back from the bathroom mirror.

What an utter failure of a day. Not only did she look a hot mess, but they'd not chopped a single stick of saleable wood. They'd have nothing to sell tomorrow except for the jars of honey she'd earned working for Carissa, unless they could trade the applesauce for something better.

The plan wasn't going as well as she had envisioned. How were they going to be independent and take care of themselves, much less bring other girls here to stay, if they couldn't even chop wood without causing bodily harm?

As she poked at her swollen features, checking for any structural damage, Emlyn screeched in the kitchen. "Olivia!"

Now what?

Afraid to find out, Olivia dashed back to the kitchen with as much speed as she could muster having with only one eye to guide her. Halfway down the hall, she met up with Emlyn. Her flailing arms and wild eyes said something was very wrong.

"It's dead. I mean… I think it's dead. I don't know how it couldn't be dead."

Olivia grasped one of the fluttering hands to get the girl to focus. "Okay, calm down. What's dead?"

The touch seemed to ground her, and Emlyn took in a breath, then blew it out. "A chicken. It must be dead. There are so many feathers… everywhere. And I only see four chickens in the shed. They've all gone to sit on top of things higher up… like they're hiding."

That wasn't good.

"Let's go see."

Olivia pulled Emlyn back through the house, out the door, and to the shed. The girl had been right. Way too many feathers were lying in clumps near the shed. Blood covered many of them.

They went into the chicken coop, and Olivia counted the remaining birds. Only four left. She felt dizzy. The weird vision of seeing out of one eye wasn't helping, but the thought of another dead bird didn't help either. She closed her remaining eye and lowered her head as she massaged her neck.

God, we could use a break here. Don't you want us to make it on our own?

After a long pause, she straightened back up and checked the nesting box. Five eggs. At least they'd gotten one more out of the fifth bird before some animal made a meal out of it. Glass half full, right?

She hugged Emlyn's shoulders. "Come on. Grab those eggs. Let's make supper."

18

Chapter Eighteen

The mirror didn't lie. Olivia's face looked like she'd lost the fight with someone huge. On the bright side, her eye was open again, though just as blackened as could be. She'd take the purple and black look over not being able to see any day.

Carissa would arrive any time now. They'd let the chickens out to forage once again, and she'd said a prayer over the silly birds asking for them to still be here when she got back. If she could find the bird netting after the market today, she'd make them an enclosure to protect them. Until then, all she could do was let them roam and pray they'd survive another day.

"Olivia." Emlyn hollered from the front door. "Someone's here."

Looking the way she did in public was disheartening, but they had jobs to do if they were going to make it on their own. So she'd pull up her big-girl panties and get to work.

Emlyn stood on the porch, waiting for her when Olivia arrived. She recognized Mr. Donahue's truck right away. Carissa was wearing her bee suit and carrying the hive box, strapped together and sealed shut.

When she saw Olivia, Carissa set the hive down and waved her over. "Where do you want it?"

Olivia jogged over to check out the newest addition to the growing arsenal she needed to feed herself and Emlyn. "I thought behind the chicken shed would be best."

"Whoa." Carissa's eyes went wide as she pulled the bee netting and hat off her face. "What happened? I hope the other guy looks worse."

"Who did that to you?" Mr. Donahue sauntered over with a low whistle. "Just let me know, and I'll kick their tail."

Emlyn had joined them by then and tentatively raised her hand. "That would be me. But I swear it was an accident."

"Carissa, Mr. Donahue, this is Emlyn—my roommate." Olivia pointed at her blackened cheek. "And this was our first lesson on how *not* to split logs."

Mr. Donahue whistled once again, louder this time, and yanked his hat off to scratch his head. "I may need to give you ladies a lesson or two in safety."

"And here I thought bees were the most dangerous activity you could get into." Carissa fit her hands to her hips, but then reached out to touch the bruise. "Do I need to get you to a doctor to check that cheek out?"

Olivia dodged the incoming hand. "No. I'm good. Let's figure out where to put the bees."

With a nod, Carissa slid her suit hood back on and picked the box up. "Lead on. As long as it's in the sun, we should be good."

None of them had suits besides Carissa, so they all watched from a respectful distance once Olivia pointed out the location. Carissa removed the straps with care and then the board covering the entrance.

She stepped back and watched the bees come and go from the hive before she joined the group. "They'll like it here. There's an extra suit for you in the truck. We can take the supplies in before we head for the market."

"I can't thank you enough for setting me up like this." Olivia stared at her new hive. "I promise I'll pay you back for everything."

"That's what we do to support each other these days, right?" Carissa gave her arm a gentle jab. "True believers are family. You've been helping me. I get to help you back."

Mr. Donahue cleared his throat. "I hate to interrupt this love fest, but I don't have time for a chorus of 'Kumbaya' right now. We need to get you to the market so I can pick up my next customer."

Carissa grinned. "Let's unload the rest of the bee supplies, and we'll head out." She started toward the truck, giving him an elbow to the ribs as she passed by. "We'll sing in the cab on the way over."

He grumbled as he followed her. "Hilarious."

At the market, they set the table up with honey jars filling the right side and applesauce on the left. Time to teach Emlyn market selling.

Olivia asked Carissa, "Do you mind if I negotiate some trades for my share of the honey and applesauce when I run sales for you?"

"By all means." Carissa waved her off with a smile. "You know what I need. I'll hold down the fort. You two go get the best deals."

Olivia removed her water thermoses from her backpack and stacked additional honey and applesauce jars in their place as

Emlyn followed her lead by adding jars to her own backpack. "Let's go. I'll introduce you to my firewood customers." Olivia poked a finger into the air. "Take a whiff and follow the scent."

Emlyn's brow furrowed as she sniffed. "Um… what?"

With a laugh, Olivia drew in a deep breath. "The smoke, silly."

How great to be back in the hunt, searching for people who burned fires at the market. Most of them were food vendors of some sort. She pointed to the air above the crowds where pillars of smoke rose.

Eyes widening, Emlyn smiled. "Oh, gotcha. Firewood customers."

Off they went, dodging in and out of the milling crowds until they reached a table with ears of corn piled in neat pyramids on one end and Mason jars filled with corn grits on the other. Behind the table stood a giant of a man, well over six and a half feet tall, bent over, stirring a kettle of water. Yellow ears of corn bobbed and boiled.

"We've got the cleanest corn you'll find here today." The woman at the table held out an ear of corn with the husk peeled back to reveal plump rows of golden kernels. She hooked a thumb toward the man behind her. "Got some hot as well if you're hungry now."

So tempting… Olivia thought of the Bible story about the man who sold his inheritance to his brother for a bowl of stew. Her stomach grumbled with desire, but she tamped the thought down.

"We've got the perfect complement to corn for your supper tonight." She set her backpack on the table and pulled out a jar of applesauce. As she displayed it, she grinned. "Wouldn't a touch of sweetness be an amazing dessert?"

The woman eyed the jar. Olivia could almost see her doing mental calculations of the value of the jar against the value of the corn ears. "Is it plain or sweetened?"

She turned up the volume on her saleswoman's smile. "It's got just a touch of honey cooked in, but it doesn't need much as the apples were sweet, to begin with."

"A dozen ears for one jar." The woman crossed her arms, a sure sign she meant it as a firm offer—nonnegotiable. "And I keep the jar without an exchange."

Swapping an empty jar when you bought a jar of food was normal protocol. It kept the jars in circulation and the production cost of the next batch down.

Olivia knew better than to assume the woman wouldn't negotiate. "Now, you know I can't let a jar go that easy." She brandished a second jar from her bag and displayed the golden honey with a flourish before setting it beside the applesauce. "Here's something to sweeten the deal, but I need grits. Three jars of yours for one honey and one applesauce… on top of two dozen ears of corn."

"That's rich." The woman scoffed. "You must think your applesauce is all that and a bag of chips if you think you're getting two dozen out of me on top of the grits."

"Oh, it's good all right. When's the last time you had sweetened applesauce?"

Olivia waited for a response while the woman stared at the jars and tapped her fingers on bony hips.

"I've never had applesauce with honey—seems like it would taste funny."

"Do you like honey?"

"Yes."

"And you like applesauce?"

"Doesn't everyone?"

Olivia swirled her finger around the rim of the honey jar to emphasize it was within her reach… if she'd only commit to the purchase. "Then what's not to love when you put the two together?"

Emlyn had hovered behind Olivia during the conversation but now stepped up to the table. "I'll bet your grits are the freshest here, just like our applesauce. Maybe you could trade us for three more of our jars, and then you could sell it with your grits—like a breakfast meal. I haven't seen anyone offer that anywhere." She lined three jars from her backpack up with the jars of grits. "Could be a big seller."

A few more seconds of finger tapping, and the woman let out a huff. "All right. I'll give you three jars of grits and two dozen corn for four jars of applesauce and one jar of honey."

"Deal," Emlyn said before Olivia could respond.

This girl was a born negotiator.

They selected the best ears and walked away, backpacks overflowing. Each of them had a hot ear, fresh out of the kettle to munch on. Neither said anything as they walked to the edge of the market area, greedily inhaling their lunch.

"I guess we should have negotiated for four jars of grits." Olivia chewed her corn. "Carissa wanted two. That leaves only one for us until the next market day."

Emlyn had swallowed her last bite. Her ear was naked from every speck of yellow. "True, but ten ears of corn should last us a while—especially if we have eggs to go with it." She tossed the empty cob in a trash barrel. "We got Carissa's grits and corn, but I haven't seen any chicken vendors yet—have you? We need to figure out how to tell if the eggs are fresh."

Olivia ran her tongue across her mouth, trying to dislodge a kernel stuck between two of her teeth as she dropped her own refuse into the waste barrel. "We're going to have to go all the way to the other end, near the auction barn, if we're going to find someone selling chickens."

They headed in that direction. She'd forgotten Nick's produce stand was in their path until they saw Anna and Brandy standing behind stacks of collard greens. Anna wasn't paying attention. She had a book in her hands. Brandy looked bored.

Olivia grasped Emlyn's arm to steer her clear of the stand, but just as she turned, she ran into a man. "Sorry. I wasn't watching where..."

Nick stood in front of her, arms crossed over his chest, glaring between her and Emlyn.

Emlyn's face blanched, and she seemed frozen in place. Olivia stepped in between them, drawing Nick's full attention to her.

Her heart raced, and her throat went dry.

"Good afternoon, ladies." His clipped words came out with controlled hostility. "It's nice to see you are healthy and safe. When you disappeared, I was afraid someone might have kidnapped you."

"We found other housing arrangements and didn't want to lose the opportunity." She tried to keep her voice light and calm, but the words came out quickly. "You know how fast properties go sometimes."

Her hand was still on Emlyn's arm, and she could feel her friend shaking.

"It can be dangerous for young ladies, such as you, to be out on their own these days." He reached out a hand and placed it on Olivia's shoulder and squeezed. Then he nodded to Emlyn.

"If your accommodations weren't to your liking, we could have worked something out."

No way was Olivia going to let him intimidate them. She took a step backward and pushed his hand off her shoulder. "We're fine on our own, thank you. Still plenty to get done today, so we'd better be going."

"You need to remember a lot of unsavory characters out there prey on young ladies." He stepped toward them, closing the gap once more. "I can keep them away from the pink house. But I can't guarantee your safety if you're not under my roof."

Was he warning her? It felt like a threat, but was it? He might only be trying to scare Emlyn, and from the vibrations running through her fingers, he was doing a good job of it.

"Thanks, but we're fine where we're at."

He brushed his fingers over Olivia's cheek, then pressed on her bruise. "I can see how fine you are with your black eye."

She'd had enough and swatted him away with her free hand. "We don't need your kind of help. I might have enough room to invite more of my friends to come live with us."

His face flushed, and his eyes flashed. Her glare better be on par with his. No way was she backing down. People were staring, and he wouldn't want to make a public spectacle.

He broke eye contact and walked past her as if he was going to his produce stand. As he passed, he stopped and growled in her ear, his hot breath feeling like an invasion. "If you come anywhere near my home or the pink house, I'll assume you want to be a permanent part of the family. I'd bet that, within a week, you'll be back, anyway. It isn't safe out there on your own. That's a guarantee."

She didn't wait for him to walk away this time. Instead, she strode in the opposite direction of his stand, pulling Emlyn along as she went.

He laughed from behind them. "You'll be back—and I'll be waiting for you."

It didn't matter if she had to grovel and beg for help from Carissa or the Worthingtons. She'd go without food to make sure Emlyn had what she needed. Neither one of them was going anywhere near Nick and his pink house ever again.

19

Chapter Nineteen

They arrived back at their sales table to find Carissa handing more honey candy out to the little urchins gathered around her. Olivia recognized Matthew from their previous meeting, and he smiled and waved as they approached. "Hey, Olivia. Remember me?"

Seeing his bright smile, she set aside her run-in with Nick to focus on the boy. "Of course, I do." She jammed her hands on her hips to give him a stern look. "Have you been behaving?"

His face flushed underneath the layer of filth, and he lowered his eyes. "Yes, ma'am."

Guilt washed over her for embarrassing him. "I'm certain you have been. It was wrong of me to ask."

She ruffled his hair, then kneeled beside him, pulling her backpack off. "I have a job that needs doing. Would you be interested in getting paid to do something for me?"

The excitement in his eyes would have been obvious from the other side of the market. "Yes, please."

Other children gathered around Carissa turned their attention to Olivia. The little girl who carried her rag doll everywhere came over and stood beside Matthew. Her words were barely audible. "Me too?"

Olivia's heart ached to hug the little pixie, so she grinned at her as she gave her tiny shoulder a gentle poke. "Of course. I'm Olivia. What's your name?"

Instead of sharing her name, the child held the doll out for Olivia to see. "This is Betsy."

With a pat on the doll's wobbly head, she used a formal voice. "It's such a pleasure to meet you, Miss Betsy."

That made the girl giggle.

Matthew bobbed from foot to foot as she fawned over the rag doll. A boy could only wait so long. He tapped her on the arm to regain her attention. "Are we going to talk about the job?"

She made a point of looking at both children as she explained the task. "I need you to find a chicken vendor. Can you do that for me?"

"Aw, that's easy. All you have to do is listen real good, and you can find 'em fast."

"Oh, but that's not the only thing I need." She put as much gravity into her voice as she could muster. "I need a chicken vendor who can answer an important question I have. Someone who knows the birds. Do you think you can find *that?*"

He twisted his lips to one side of his face and stared at the ground. Then the little girl stood on her tiptoes and whispered in his ear. A grin broke out on his face, but he tamped it back down and put a serious face on. "We can do that. What does the job pay?"

She bit her lip to stifle a smile, then fought to respond without snickering. "We should negotiate for food. What do you think of one jar of applesauce each?"

The little girl's eyes lit up, and she hopped up and down. "Yes."

Matthew didn't look quite as convinced. "A whole jar for each of us? And no trade-ins? I don't have any empty jars."

She stood up and dusted the dirt off her knees. "You drive a hard bargain, sir—but I accept your terms."

"Whoo-hoo!" the boy hooted, and they both took off into the market crowd.

By the time she turned to Carissa, the children had all disappeared, and Emlyn stood behind the table hugging her arms around her chest.

"That was sweet of you," Carissa said, then touched Emlyn's hand. "You look like you've had a fright. Is everything okay?"

Before Emlyn could say anything, Olivia jumped in. "Just some creep we ran into. But we got rid of him."

All Emlyn would do was nod and avoid eye contact.

Olivia stepped behind the table and opened her backpack. "We got your corn and grits and some of our own as well. We'll leave what we got here with you before we go out again."

Carissa picked up an ear of corn. "It's getting late for corn. You were lucky to find some. If you can get some cabbages and plenty of salt, I'll teach you how to make sauerkraut."

After putting her purchases in the hard plastic cooler, Olivia loaded more applesauce and honey into her backpack. Emlyn hadn't moved a muscle. "Are you going to unpack your load?"

Emlyn dropped onto the cooler's closed lid. "If it's okay with you, I'll stay here with Carissa."

Was her friend so spooked by what Nick had said that she'd be afraid to work the market? Perhaps she just needed a minute to collect her thoughts. "You wait for the kids to come back.

Get the information from them, and I'll be back soon."

If she was going to make this happen, she needed to find Jan Worthington and ask her about lessons in raising rabbits. They'd be at the far end of the market, as usual, tending to their table as well as the food pantry.

In this time of food scarcity, when people needed it the most, it surprised her some people still cared enough to give away what little surplus they could eke out of the ground. Of course, the Worthington farm was no wimpy production. They raised beef cattle and grew crops year-round. They gathered with their neighbors to preserve as much as they could and then shared what they had with others.

Olivia wanted to do that herself someday. But today, she'd be happy not to starve along with Emlyn.

Using her power-walking steps, Olivia made it across the market with enough time, she hoped, to speak with Jan and still have time to get the answers she needed about eggs.

Her heart surprised her by jumping into her throat when Olivia sighted the Worthington family behind their table. It felt like ages, instead of mere months, since she'd last worked with them.

Caleb stood at the end of the table. His dark hair had grown longer than she remembered. The uncut bangs hid one eye while he spoke to a customer. Jan handed a Mason jar of beans to a woman with two little ones hanging on her skirts. It was hard to tell whether Jan was working for the food pantry or their own sales table. Must be their sales table though, as the longer line was at a second stand just steps away, where Mrs. Worthington stood with her two neighbors.

Olivia averted her gaze from that line and the temptation to go to the food pantry table and get some extra food until they got on their feet. But she didn't have enough time to stand in that line, then talk to Jan, and still make it back to talk to the chicken vendor.

Jan's face lit up when they made eye contact. She screeched "Olivia!" and ran from the table to hug her.

The embrace practically melted Olivia. As soon as the embrace ended, she admitted, "I've missed you."

"I told Caleb I'd seen you here." Jan grabbed her by the arm and hauled her back to the sales table where Caleb waited on his customer. "He misses you too—and *what* happened to your face?"

Olivia's free hand twitched to touch the forgotten-about bruise. "Me versus a ricocheting mallet while splitting logs. I'm sure you can guess who won."

The moment Caleb finished his transaction, he eyed her, his eyes dimming. "Long time, no see. You okay?"

His smile made her knees go weak. It was hard to look into his blue eyes, so she dodged them by picking up one of the wooden wolf whistles he carved for sale.

"Hey, Caleb. I'm good."

Just then, another customer came up to him. "I love your bowls, but can you make a special order?"

Caleb gave her one last smile before facing the customer. "Of course, let's talk specifics."

Jan whisked her back to the golf cart behind their table. "Let's get away from the table and catch up for a minute. Shall we? What have you been up to?"

Olivia scrambled into the rear seat beside her friend. "I was hoping you could help me out with something. I want to raise rabbits. Can you teach me?"

A snicker was Jan's first response. "Of course, I'm happy to.

But I'll be honest. Jacob is the rabbit whisperer. He's fixated on the creatures and knows more about them than any of us know at this point. He's got so many now that he's planning to sell them at the market soon."

"Already? Didn't he just get started?"

"Exactly! But he's already had to buy unrelated mates for his litters." The smile on her face seemed like an inside joke. "There's a reason people joke about multiplying like rabbits."

The timing couldn't have been more perfect. "I'll be his first customer. Do you think I could come over to see the ones he wants to sell?"

"Of course, you're always welcome at our place. I've told you that."

Olivia nodded in Caleb's direction. "I wasn't positive he'd want me around. You know—after what Rob did."

Jan's shoulders slumped. Then she sat up straighter and waved toward her brother as if to say "just look at him now."

"He's dealing with it. Took him a while to let go of what Rob did. Then he went to visit Rob last week, but they weren't home. He wants to reconcile. They've been friends for as long as I can remember."

Should she tell Jan about the family taking Rob to rehab? Probably best to wait until he returned. If he returned.

"Well, I've still got one last errand to run before today ends, so I need to get going." She pulled Jan into another embrace. "I miss you, and I'm going to take you up on your offer to visit. Expect me soon."

She dashed back to her table on the other side of the market and found Matthew waiting.

The moment he saw her coming, he jumped up and ran to her. "I found it. Someone who knows everything about chickens."

"Excellent! Take me there."

He was hard to follow as he dodged through tight spots, evading adults. Twice, she lost him in the crowds, and he doubled back and grabbed her hand. Sure enough, they soon arrived at a table surrounded by chicken pens full of chicks. They also sold supplies, including feed, waterers, and netting.

"I just have a quick question," she said to the rail-thin man behind the table. "How can I tell if eggs I find are fresh or not?"

The man spit a mouthful of dark goo on the ground. "Simple. Put them in a bucket of water. If they sink and lay flat… they're still good. Floaters need to be tossed."

So simple. She smiled gratefully. "Thanks!"

Now they'd be able to use at least some of those eggs. She was sure of it.

They returned to their table once more, and she paid both children, then helped Carissa pack up the few unsold jars. It had been a productive, exhausting, and thought-provoking day. They were all ready to go home.

Mr. Donahue gave them a lift back to their respective homes, and both were dragging by the time they sat in the kitchen to empty their backpacks. Ears of corn, along with jars of grits, applesauce, and honey, filled their pantry. A good day's work. Checking the eggs was a task for tomorrow. They were making progress. Given time, they'd survive on their own just fine.

"I'm going to grab the eggs and secure the chickens in the shed for the evening," she said to Emlyn. The sun had begun its descent. "Just want to have applesauce again? I think we can get the fire pit ready to go tomorrow if we can collect some wood."

Emlyn nodded. "And I'll be more careful this time. I

promise."

Olivia smiled and then went out to pick up the day's eggs and close the shed. It was another night with no power, so she needed to get them tucked away before it grew too dark to see. The feathers from the dead bird seemed to have multiplied as she drew closer to the coop. The more she saw, the more uneasy she felt.

Something wasn't right.

Tools, bags, and other items from the shed were lying outside among the feathers.

As she ducked inside, she saw only one chicken, and the shed's contents were strewn about as if a mini tornado had blown through. The nest held only broken shells. Something had gotten the chickens—again. Only this time, very little was left.

Stepping back outside, she eyed the familiar wooden pieces among the feathers and other debris. She bent down and picked one up. Part of a beehive frame.

Oh no. Not the bees.

She ran around to the building's opposite side and gasped at what she feared she'd see. Something had torn the beehive apart, leaving bits of honeycomb and frame debris strewn everywhere. Scratches covered the outside of the broken box. Something big must've found the hive and couldn't resist the sweet treat any more than humans could.

Now what? Wild animals had ruined everything.

Tears flowed down her face as she trudged back to the shed and closed the one remaining bird in.

Sobs followed a bitter laugh. She dropped to her knees in front of the door.

Why?

She bowed her head. "What did I do, God? I don't understand. Do you hate me that much? Not even a few more eggs before you take it all away?"

She was done.

"Olivia?"

Emlyn's blurry outline filtered through Olivia's tears. Then a fresh bout of sobs overtook her when Emlyn kneeled beside her.

"What is it?" Emlyn cooed as she clamped a hand on Olivia's shoulder. "What happened?"

Olivia pulled herself together enough to sum it up for her friend. "It's over. Gone. No chickens. No bees. No eggs. Nothing."

A horrible end of a horrendous day.

20

Chapter Twenty

What was the point of pushing herself if everything fell apart in the end? Olivia couldn't think of even one thing that had gone her way since the variant took her mother.

Dad chose alcohol over her.

Rob did the same and took her only remaining family with him.

Carissa had given up a beehive to allow her a chance to care for them, and some animal had wiped them out on the first day.

The chickens she'd worked so hard for and bartered for were all gone except for one.

She didn't even have eggs left for dinner until they checked each one from the old pile.

The worst part was Emlyn. Olivia promised her they could make it on their own. And this was what her friend got for following along—dead birds, dead bees, a big, fat dead end.

"I'm sorry." The words came out soggy through the tears she couldn't swallow back. "I've let you down."

"Aw, come on." Emlyn tugged on her arm, pulling her up and toward the house. "No sense sitting out here crying about it. You've worked so hard. This is just a setback. You'll see."

Once they were in the house, Emlyn sat Olivia across the kitchen table from her. Olivia's bruised cheek ached as much as her heart. All she could think was that, if there was a God, he must hate her or feel indifferent to her pleas.

Remembering her mother, she knew what Mom would say right now. *"Let's pray about it."*

She huffed out a bitter laugh.

"What?" A glimmer of a smile curved Emlyn's cheeks. "Share with the rest of the class. You can't keep something funny in. We could both use cheering up."

"It's nothing. I was just thinking about my mom. She was a Christian. If she were still alive, we'd be praying about this whole mess right now."

Emlyn arched her eyebrows. "So why aren't you?"

"Like it's doing me any good. Look at where it's gotten me." Olivia swirled her hand in the air as if to encompass her universe. "Nowhere."

"So that's it?" Emlyn's nostrils flared as she glared. "You're quitting? What about the other girls? Did you see Anna and Brandy today at that produce stand? Nick was selling them. You don't even care enough to keep going for them?"

Olivia slammed her palm on the table so hard it would probably bruise to match her face. "What do you want from me? I can't keep chickens alive, and you want me to keep an entire house full of people going?" Leaning in toward Emlyn, she flattened her hands on the table and pushed herself from her chair. "We're going to be eating applesauce for supper for a while now. Eggs won't be a menu staple with only one chicken left."

The ever-elusive electricity surged into the house, turning on a light above their heads, creating a hum in the empty refrigerator, and generating a blinking 12:00 on the stove clock.

"Hmm. I get the feeling someone heard you." Emlyn stood and walked over to their meager pantry and pulled out a jar. "And we're having grits for supper… with honey."

Olivia couldn't believe the power would return. Perhaps God was paying attention, at least a little.

«»

As they walked to Carissa's home the next day, Olivia bantered with herself about what she'd say. Should she just come out with "Sorry, but I killed your bees" or perhaps "Remember that hive you left me?" No matter what she came up with, it was all still an admission of failure. Her failure.

She hadn't a clue what had gotten into Emlyn, though. Apparently, seeing someone else fall apart was all she needed to turn into "Polly Positive." She'd woke at dawn, bounced into Olivia's room, and roused her out of bed. "Let's go to Carissa's and get started on another batch of applesauce. Tomorrow, we'll try chopping wood again."

Now, as they walked, Emlyn kept chattering about anything and everything. She didn't seem to care that Olivia was stuck in her own head or that she was having a one-sided conversation.

"You couldn't ask for a prettier fall day, could you?" Emlyn continued to spout. "We should bring back some extra apples for the rabbits you wanted to buy from the Worthingtons. Whatcha think?"

So now, Emlyn wanted to raise rabbits. When Olivia mentioned it the day before, Emlyn had been squeamish about having to "kill a bunny." Who was this girl walking with her, and what had she done with the fearful Emlyn?

Olivia picked up her pace as if she were in a speed-walking contest and Emlyn was the person to beat.

"Applesauce, rabbits, firewood, bees… I thought you said we couldn't make it on our own. Now you're doubling down on what I said we could do in the first place? And this is after we lost all but one chicken and the beehive?"

"Aw, stop it." Emlyn jogged to catch up, her butterfly bun slipping. "You're the one who's been saying we could do this. Don't give up on me. Or on the other girls."

Olivia stopped, causing Emlyn to stop short of running into her.

"Those girls don't want to leave Nick and his pretty pink house." Heat roiled in Olivia like a volcano about to erupt. "If they did, they'd be out of there already, just like us."

Emlyn's face flared as red as a fire engine. She glared like Olivia had just kicked a puppy dog. "You don't get it, do you? People have let those girls down and abandoned them so many times they feel worthless. The only person who says they have value is Nick. And you know what he thinks they're worth."

Olivia had to look away from the fury in Emlyn's eyes, but Emlyn wasn't done yet. She advanced toward Olivia, poking a finger at her and thumping it into her sternum to emphasize the next words.

"Stella and Molly have worked for Nick for so long, they think it's the only way they can survive." She jabbed her words and finger at Olivia again. "Deep down, Lilly and Ruby know what Nick wants from them, so they're hiding behind the oblivion of drugs." Another poke. "Anna hides in her books, and Brandy clings to Anna, hoping not to be alone in the end."

A final jab, then a solid push backward with her palm. "At least you're not *afraid* to be independent. That's what made me think I could do it too. Until now."

Emlyn turned on her heel and stalked off toward Carissa's house.

Olivia's face continued to burn, but her anger had fizzled to shame. She'd convinced Emlyn to follow her, persuaded her they could make it on their own, and then given up on both of them. The knot forming in her gut twisted.

They made the rest of their brisk walk in silence. She wanted to apologize but couldn't figure out how to fix things. She had to get them back on track. But, how?

Smoke rose behind Carissa's house when they arrived. They went around to the back to investigate, and as she came into view, Carissa placed a log on the fire. A kettle rested beside the flames.

"Hello, again." Emlyn pranced over to the fire pit. "Can't wait to learn how this all works."

The two embraced as if they were best friends who'd been apart for years. The old happy-happy joy-joy Emlyn had returned.

Olivia fisted her hands at her side, her clenched teeth grinding together. Why couldn't she let the previous day's failures go the way Emlyn had?

"You ready too?" Carissa pulled Olivia into a side hug, seeming to understand she wasn't feeling her companion's excitement. "Or do we need to chat first?"

Since when did Carissa suggest a conversation before work? "Chat about what?"

Carissa's hands joined her hips, and her brows rose. "About whatever has gotten under your skin and vamped your friend up to the supersonic level." Carissa eyed Emlyn. "You two have a fight or something?"

Ignoring the pleading in Emlyn's eyes wasn't easy, but the last thing Olivia wanted to do was lay her failures out to her mentor for viewing. At least if she explained, she could control the story better than Emlyn would.

She let out a breath. "I lost the bees—and all the chickens but one."

Carissa took a step toward her, slipped her hands off her hips, and reached out to Olivia's shoulders. "I'm so sorry. That's rotten luck."

Luck? More like failure. Olivia could feel her eyebrows furrowing as Emlyn jumped in before she could respond.

"It was unfortunate. And she's been working so hard too."

Yes. She'd worked hard. They were supposed to be making progress every day, not one step forward and then two steps back. They didn't have time for mistakes.

The tears pooled, but she refused to let them fall. She pinched the skin between her thumb and pointer finger. Painful, but effective in redirecting her attention.

"No matter." Carissa started toward the shed, pulling Olivia along with her. "We'll get you another hive. Let's talk about what happened so we can prevent it next time."

"No." Olivia edged back. It wasn't Carissa's fault that an animal had torn the beehives apart. Olivia hadn't done enough work to earn a second hive. "I'll get another hive when I've learned more. Let's get to work. Okay?"

Carissa paused and stared at her.

The look felt invasive—as if Carissa were digging into her soul, searching for something. Olivia had to look away.

Moments later, a quiet voice spoke. "What's going on?"

Carissa stood inches away from her… deep in Olivia's personal space.

Olivia stepped back a pace and focused on the ground. "It's nothing."

"Nothing? It's something—a big something."

Emlyn's arm encircled her waist. "She feels like she failed. But I keep telling her it isn't true. We can make a place for all of us to live. She just needs her confidence back."

Olivia glared at her friend. Her former friend. The one she thought knew how to keep a confidence.

"And who exactly does 'all of us' entail?" Carissa focused in on Emlyn now. "Olivia doesn't talk much about her family and friends."

Emlyn's face flushed, and she shifted her weight from foot to foot as if she were standing on hot coals. "Well, we…"

Just great. Olivia jumped in before Emlyn could overexplain. "It's just friends of ours. We wanted to invite them to live with us, is all."

"You two look as cagey as a pickpocket eyeing his mark." The hands slammed back to the hips, and a no-nonsense look reserved for mothers settled in her eyes. "Let's hear the entire story, shall we?"

Then it happened—a flood of words—not hers, but Emlyn's.

"Nick invites girls to live at the pink house. He seems all nice, like he's doing you a favor, but then there's drugs and favors and dates and creepy guys." Emlyn paused long enough to take a quick breath. "And then Molly came home with a black eye and a bloody lip. I didn't want to believe it, but Stella said Nick hit her. Olivia said I could live with her. I didn't think it was possible, because we're just girls, you know. But she's amazing, and she has all these ideas. But Nick said if we go back, he'll assume we want to live there permanently, but the other girls are still there. And Lilly and Ruby never came back from the last party, but…"

Olivia clamped a hand over Emlyn's mouth to stop the spewing, which caused Emlyn's eyes to go wide. Carissa's sun-goldened face had blanched.

Olivia jerked her hand back. Emlyn pursed her lips into a straight line and drew her fingers across her lips in a zipping motion.

Too late. The information was out there.

Carissa shook her head in slow motion, long black hair swooshing with the movement. "Do I understand correctly that this Nick character is luring young girls into drugs and sex with men they don't know?" She looked each of them in the eye. When they didn't respond, she clamped her hands into fists at her sides. "Where is he? Where is this pink house?"

This was what Olivia hadn't wanted. She didn't want to embarrass her friends. She didn't want Carissa or anyone else looking down on them because they took Nick up on his offer. She wanted to give them another way to live—a way to escape.

Time to take control of the situation again.

"I've got it under control." She stalked toward the shed to collect her apple picker. "I just need to get a few more things settled. Then I can invite them to live with us."

Then Emlyn unlocked those cute but loose lips once more. "But Nick said…"

It took only one flash of anger directed at the blabbermouth to stop her midsentence. Emlyn jammed her hands into her jeans pockets, rocked back on her heels, and tipped her face to the sky.

"We're fine." Olivia growled. "It's under control."

"Look." Carissa held up a hand, pleading in her eyes. "I don't know why you feel as if you must do this on your own. But you don't. You have friends, like me, who care and can help. Being independent doesn't mean being alone."

The same pleading look darkened Emlyn's gray eyes.

They were ganging up on her. Not fair.

Olivia wanted to turn back toward the shed, grab the picker, and figure this out on her own.

"Please?" It was almost a whisper from Emlyn as she put her hands together in a prayerful, begging motion.

Something inside Olivia broke. A voice in her head urged her to accept the offer.

"This is the way," the voice said. *"Together. Not alone."*

"Fine," she said to Emlyn. Then to Carissa, "Nick. He seems like a nice guy. But he's not."

And she told Carissa everything.

21

Chapter Twenty-One

Olivia hated the concern in Carissa's eyes that grew deeper by the minute. Somehow, putting what she knew into words made the situation even more real. Her friends' position didn't seem as bad in her head, but as she explained it all to Carissa, the truth was painful.

"The oldest, Molly and Stella, are so used to their life, I don't think they'll leave, even if I can prove we can support ourselves. Not sure about Ruby and Lilly, either." She nudged Emlyn. "But I think Anna and Brandy would come with us, don't you?"

"I'm not sure." Emlyn rubbed her biceps, arms crossed over her chest. "Being on our own is still scary to think about sometimes. At least with Nick, we never went hungry." Her face flushed with her apparent realization of what she'd said. "Sorry. I should add that he fed us if we did what we were told."

Olivia thought back to her punishment for disobeying Nick. "Precisely."

"Why didn't you girls tell me what was going on?" Carissa rubbed her temples, her words emerging with a combination of pleading and cajoling. "You had to know I would help. I wouldn't let you starve."

"I was afraid of what you'd think of us." Olivia couldn't look Carissa in the eye. "I mean, I never made it to one of Nick's parties, but that's where I was headed. And my friends did what they thought they had to in order to survive."

"It's embarrassing." Emlyn kept her head ducked, her face still flushed. "I don't think I could have survived at that party without the drugs and alcohol making everything fuzzy. I'm glad I don't remember most of it. The bits I remember weren't nice."

By the end of her sentence, Emlyn's voice had diminished to a whisper.

That was it. Olivia wasn't going to let Nick scare her off, but she had to be smart at the same time.

"I've got my uncle's home to myself right now, but if they come back, I need to know there's a place for everyone. Can some of the girls stay with you if that happens?" She waved back at the cozy home, then raised both hands. "Only temporarily, of course."

"I'd have taken all of you in if I'd known what was going on." Carissa pulled Olivia into a quick side hug, then released her. "From what you're telling me, we're going to need more people in our corner. Who else knows about this that we can rely on?"

That question had been marinating in her brain for a while now. Now, it was time for her to answer. "I've got an idea."

Could she trust again? She'd been a hot mess—hopelessly afraid of being alone after her father abandoned her. All she'd wanted was for someone to care for her.

Somehow, that had evolved into her taking the lead. Wrapped up in Rob's problems, her aunt and uncle couldn't take care of themselves, much less be there to support her.

Then she remembered back to before the alcohol had consumed her family's lives. Back to when she'd spent time at the Worthington farm. She'd heard the stories of when the marauders had come to the farm trying to take what didn't belong to them.

The Worthingtons gathered their neighbors and fought back. As a group.

Later, circumstances tested the group's unity once more. Rob's betrayal caused Caleb's past to be used against him—separating him from his family. But once he fessed up, they'd all come together again to support him.

Even more importantly, the Worthingtons hadn't just supported their own. They took in the siblings of the girl who blackmailed them.

They were Christians. Mrs. Worthington, the strongest of all. They displayed Bible verses, crosses, and encouraging sayings all over their house. Though Mr. Worthington wasn't as demonstrative about his faith, he supported his wife in hers.

If they could take in the children of someone who'd attacked them, they'd help her out.

The rest of the day they worked in the orchard, then processed the apples into a long line of gleaming applesauce-filled jars. While they worked, they planned until they had a solid strategy.

«»

Olivia had forgotten how long the Worthingtons' driveway was. A half-mile dirt-and-stone private road led back into the woods. Or at least it appeared you were heading into the woods. If she hadn't been here before, she'd have been creeped out at the isolation. It felt as though she was heading toward a backwater hick's shack.

"Are you sure it's safe back here?" Emlyn, having accompanied Olivia, was looking more nervous the farther up the driveway they went. "If I hear banjos playing, I'm turning around."

Olivia laughed. "It's not banjos you have to worry about with the Worthingtons. It's explosives and booby traps."

Emlyn stopped short, grabbed Olivia's arm, and spun her on her heel. "Explosives?"

"It's a long story." She peeled Emlyn's iron grip off her wrist and gave her a gentle tug to get them moving again. "I haven't seen any signs. They gave plenty of warning last time they set traps. We'll be fine. I promise."

At least I'm pretty sure we're fine.

She was almost positive the two people who blackmailed Caleb were the last of the marauder group that attacked the Worthington farm. Rob hadn't mentioned any other gang members once he confessed his involvement and ratted out the two he'd been working with.

They'd gone down a hill in the driveway and were coming up the other side when the woods opened to reveal huge fenced-in pastures, a farmhouse, and multiple pole barns and sheds, as well as cattle and gardens. A chicken coop rested in the field beside the home, and as they drew closer to the house, she sighted the greenhouse farther on.

Seeing the farm again sent bees zooming around in her stomach. She'd be able to see her friends, perhaps even Caleb. Who knew what the reception would be, but at least, she would know—one way or another.

A sound coming closer turned the nervous flutters into spikes of terror. Barking dogs charged them. Emlyn clamped onto her wrist, practically cutting off her circulation.

"I don't like dogs." Her nervous voice, combined with her backpedaling promised her terror was real. "Let's go."

"Wait." Olivia put her hand over the other girl's to calm her. "They're just letting the family know we're here… I think."

The dogs came tearing out of the woods in their direction, following a fence line.

"Hello!" She hollered toward the house. "Anybody home?"

She wasn't sure what the dogs would do once they reached them. Should they stand their ground? Would the dogs calm once they arrived? Her heart pounded, and Emlyn's nails dug into her arm.

A clanging came from the house. Someone stood on the front porch, smacking the triangle dangling from one corner.

Her taut muscles sagged. "It's okay." She hugged Emlyn. "That's their dinner and alarm bell. They know we're here."

"Max… Luna… off!"

An electric golf cart headed toward them from the direction opposite of the dogs. The animals' reaction was instantaneous. Heeding their master's order, the dogs stopped barking and sat.

"Good morning, ladies." Caleb waved as he stopped the cart beside them. "It's good to see you again, Olivia. Let me give you a ride to the house."

"This is Emlyn." Olivia pulled her friend into the cart's second seat behind Caleb. "She's not a fan of dogs."

"Now that they've seen us together, they won't be a problem." He drove toward the house. "It's great to meet you, Emlyn. Jan's in the house with Mom—canning the last of the bean crop. They'll be excited to see you again."

Sitting behind Caleb brought back memories of her time spent with the family. Being a part of the neighborhood had been so much fun, like being part of a large family where they all got together to share work and meals. They'd even started the food pantry together. Most importantly, they'd defended the farm as one. She needed that now.

They arrived at the front porch, and Jan stood at the top, beaming and bouncing in place as if cheering them on.

"It's about time you showed up." Jan opened the door and ushered them inside. "We could have used an extra set of hands picking the beans. Head for the kitchen."

Familiar smells made Olivia's heart do a little flip. It had been so long since she'd been in this house, working shoulder to shoulder with the team. The familiar scents of canning and other more heavenly aromas floated past. They'd had cornbread and pinto beans recently. Or perhaps, that was the next meal.

Her stomach growled—loud and gurgling—just as Mrs. Worthington pulled her into a hug.

"Olivia, it's so good to see you." After the generous squeeze, Mrs. Worthington pushed her back at arm's length and appraised her. "You're too skinny. We'll have to fatten you up a smidge."

Then she grasped Emlyn's hand, drawing her into her warmth. "And who might this lovely young lady be?"

Oops. Lost in reminiscing, Olivia had forgotten her friend. "Sorry. This is my roommate, Emlyn."

"It's so nice to meet you, honey. Come on in and grab a seat." Mrs. Worthington pointed to the stools. "Jan, get our company some of those muffins. I'm sure Jacob didn't inhale *all* of them."

Jacob. She couldn't wait to see him again. His enthusiasm was contagious. The house had to be overflowing with people by now, but it was too quiet for the number she knew had been living here.

Three other kids besides Jacob lived here now. "Where's everybody?"

An old-fashioned wind-up timer rang. Jan picked it up to silence it, then turned off the pressure cooker on the stove. "They're all over at the food pantry, getting it organized for this weekend's giveaway. This is the last of the bean crop, and it'll go over there tomorrow as well."

That explained it. The entire neighborhood chipped in to help. Her family used to be part of that—until Rob ruined everything.

Jan set a plate of muffins in front of them. Flatter than the ones Olivia's mom used to buy from the store, they still wafted an enticing blueberry scent.

It was all she could do to tamp down her desire to shovel the entire plate into her mouth. "Thank you."

"Are those blueberries?" Emlyn pulled one apart and inhaled. "Oh my, yes."

Neither of them said another word until two of the muffins had disappeared. Jan brought them water, and they sipped, staring at the remaining treats on the plate.

"Now, don't be shy." Mrs. Worthington pushed the plate toward them. "If you don't eat them, Jacob will. And he already had more than his fair share."

Olivia joined Emlyn in selecting a second, but she restrained herself, plucked a piece off, and popped it into her mouth instead of wolfing it down. After she swallowed, she needed to get to the point.

"I know there's bad blood between our families now, but I hoped you'd help us with a problem."

Mrs. Worthington's eyebrows furrowed, and she stepped

to Jan's side, the two sharing a look before the older woman faced Olivia. "No, honey. There's no problem between us. What happened was between Rob and Caleb. That wasn't your doing." She wiped her hands on a towel, then placed it on the counter, flattening it over and over as if she were trying to iron it with her palms. "I hope you haven't stayed away because of that. Caleb feels bad enough, as it is, telling Rob not to come over."

Heat prickled behind Olivia's eyes, and pent-up air whooshed from her lungs. This was what she'd hoped to hear, what she'd expected. But having it confirmed empowered her to take the next step.

"We need help—the help of the entire team who fought off the marauders. Friends of ours are in trouble, and I have a plan. But we need the support of your family and neighbors to make it work."

"This sounds serious." Mrs. Worthington stopped smoothing the already wrinkle-free towel and touched Jan's arm. "Ring the bell again. Give it some extra emphasis this time. Let's bring the men home to hear this."

Chapter Twenty-Two

Olivia was going to vomit at any moment. Was she insane for even trying this? It had seemed like an amazing plan when she'd talked everyone into it.

The entire gang—Worthington family, friends, and neighbors had listened to what was going on at the pink house. Even Emlyn contributed what she remembered from the party she'd attended.

Once they understood what was at risk, they agreed to join in and bring all their resources to support her and the girls under Nick's control.

Over the next days, they'd gotten the plan's pieces into place for the craziest game Olivia had ever played. This contest was for keeps, and she was terrified she'd say or do the wrong thing and ruin it for everyone.

Mrs. Worthington led them in prayer this morning before they'd left to play their roles. Before Olivia could leave, Mrs. Worthington pulled her aside for a private chat.

"Now you know I'm going to be praying for you every second you're out of my sight." She sat on the couch beside Olivia.

Her hand rested on an embroidery loop while she smoothed a plain white pillowcase out in her lap. "I won't stop until I can wrap my arms around you in the biggest hug you've ever experienced."

Olivia held back tears, sensing her mother was there with her in Mrs. Worthington's words. "Yes, ma'am. I appreciate that. I'm going to be praying too—if I can keep my attention on it."

The older woman nodded. "Perfect." She tapped the empty loop on the pillowcase. "I work with my hands when I'm stressed. Helps me to concentrate on my prayers. So, I'm starting a special project. Do you, by any chance, have a favorite Bible verse?"

Her mother's passage popped into her head as if carrying a message from God. He was on her side today. The side of those who wanted good in the world, fighting against the Nicks who brought harm.

"Galatians 5:1."

Mrs. Worthington's face almost glowed, and her shoulders relaxed. "That seems perfect for today, doesn't it? What's your favorite color?"

"Today, it's blue. Like the open sky and the untamable ocean at peace. The color of freedom."

Mrs. Worthington gave Olivia one last squeeze before she left for her long walk.

Caleb had offered to drive her most of the way, and it had been so tempting to take him up on it. His demeanor had been so serious once he'd heard their story. It was as if something in him had switched on, and he was in full protection mode. But she needed a clear head, and the time to walk would accomplish that. Plus, it wouldn't do for someone at Nick's to see her dropped off.

Emlyn wanted to come with her today, but that wasn't part of the plan. If Olivia had to worry about the girl saying something she shouldn't the entire day, she'd never be able to concentrate. Best to have fewer pawns in the game for Nick to play with.

When the pink house came into view, she paused. This was it. Even if the plan went all kinds of wrong, once she knocked on that door, the twisted game would begin. If she were going to back down and try something else, this was the moment.

Something brushed her legs. She jumped, letting out a squeal, then clapped a hand over her mouth to silence herself. Sam, Emlyn's cat, was staring up at her. "Ooh." Her knees wobbled, and she squatted to pet her as she purred. "Sorry, we couldn't come back for you. But if I have any say in the matter, you're coming home with me tonight. Emlyn would love to see you again."

The cat pushed her head into Olivia's palm, demanding more attention and running her purr-motor at full tilt.

"You're a good excuse to go knock on that door. Thanks, Sam."

Scooping the cat off the ground, Olivia proceeded to the pink house's front porch and rapped on the door.

It took forever for the door to open. Olivia nearly dropped the cat when Nadine was the one standing there. Nadine's eyes narrowed, and she whispered, "What are you doing here?"

Olivia held the cat out in front of her. "Sam found me. I thought I'd bring her back."

Nadine stepped onto the porch, ignoring the animal, and pulled the door shut behind her with a gentle click. "You don't seem to understand you can't just waltz up to this house anytime you like. Are you insane or stupid?"

Why hadn't she understood before? Nadine tried to protect her from becoming one of Nick's girls right from the beginning. Olivia had been a blind idiot. Could she trust Nadine, or was she in too deep with Nick to be an ally?

This might be the woman's last chance to choose a side. Olivia needed to know what Nadine's intentions were. "I'm neither. But what about you? Why are you here? What does Nick have over you?"

"You don't understand—"

"Nadine?" A man's voice bellowed from the other side of the door. "Who's here?"

"Go." Nadine shoved Olivia, her eyes wild.

The door opened before Olivia could react, and Nick stood before her.

The moment he recognized her, his eyebrows went up along with his lips. "Well, now, who do we have here? Has our feisty guest returned—decided it's better to have food in her belly than the freedom to run wild?"

His hand struck as fast as a rattlesnake, grabbed her arm, and towed her into the house. Nadine squeezed her eyes shut as Olivia passed her, refusing to make eye contact.

Well, she was in it now—too late to back out. Things were progressing as planned—which was what she wanted. She hoped.

He dragged her into the living room where it appeared they'd been meeting. He shoved her into the middle. As familiar faces gawked at her from couches and chairs, he laughed. "Look who's back in time for tonight's party. And what happened to that pretty face of yours? Someone got you good."

The couch was full. Anna sat with a book clutched in her lap, Brandy beside her, leaning in. As Olivia expected, Carissa sat on the opposite end, her hair pulled back into a ponytail, which made her look much younger.

Olivia averted her gaze, careful not to greet her. As far as Nick and everyone else in the room knew, they were strangers. Carissa'd done her part to be in the room—supposedly another fool who fell into Nick's trap.

Molly sat in the overstuffed chair while Stella perched on its arm. The sadness in Molly's eyes was like a gut punch, but Stella's sneer fortified Olivia. "Didn't think I'd see you again. Idiot."

"Now, now… we're all friends in this room," Nick said to Stella. "Olivia just wanted to be reunited with her family."

Nadine wandered into the room. A frown dragged the edges of her mouth downward. "It's almost time for guests to arrive," she said to Nick. "I'd better get back to the house to greet them."

He clapped his hands and rubbed them together. "That's your prompt to get ready, ladies. The party awaits your lovely presences."

They rose from their places and filtered out of the room.

"Stella, I'm certain you can find something for Olivia to wear?" He nodded to the animal in her arms. "Get rid of that thing."

Carissa passed by, and to keep from looking at her, Olivia followed Stella up to the older girl's second-floor bedroom. Stella's angry strides slowed once she was in the room. Then she jammed her hands on her hips and advanced on Olivia. "Why? Why would you come back after you'd gotten away?"

Olivia had forgotten the cat was in her arms until it hissed in response to Stella's aggression, then jumped free, and sprinted down the hallway.

CHAPTER TWENTY-TWO

Too bad she couldn't follow Sam. She had the safer plan.

"It's difficult out there on your own." She'd practiced saying the words, wanting them to come out naturally. "I thought Emlyn and I could make it together."

"Well, at least she was smart enough not to come back here." Stella yanked open her dresser drawer and pulled clothing out, flinging it everywhere in angry fits. "You hadn't even been to one of Nick's parties yet. You could have gotten away clean."

Olivia bit into her tongue, stifling the urge to confess the entire plan. But she couldn't be sure how deep Stella was in. Would she side with Nick after all this time?

Best to say nothing. Just play the game.

Having flung a good portion of the drawer's contents around the room, Stella put her hands on top of the dresser, lowered her head between her arms, then huffed. After rubbing her eyes, she stood back up, then shook her head. "Whatever."

Turning to face Olivia, she tossed two scraps of fabric at her. She scooped up a pair of jean shorts from the floor and threw them too. "Those'll work. Get changed. It's your debut night—pool party at the big house."

Olivia's clutch on the two scraps loosened. Great. The scraps were the top and bottom of a micro bikini. She'd never seen something so flimsy. What was the point? "Um... Do you have anything a bit more... substantial?"

Stella barked out a laugh. "Get used to it, kiddo. After you get a few of Nick's parties under your belt, that'll feel downright matronly."

Holding the suit out in front of her, Olivia shivered over how cheap the girls who wore them must have felt the first time. Her cheeks warmed. "I'll... I'll go to the bathroom to change."

"Really?" Stella rolled her eyes. "You can change in here. Just meet me in the kitchen for your pregame relaxer."

Stella slammed the door as she swept out of the room.

Olivia listened to the retreating stomps until they were gone.

This was it. Once she put the suit on and showed up in the kitchen, there was no backing down. She laid the clothes on the bed, smoothed out the tiny top and bottom, then the jeans shorts beside them.

Woman up. Let's get this show on the road.

She pulled off her T-shirt and bra, then tied the bikini top behind her back and around her neck. It was probably a stupid move, but she double knotted the strings as if a double knot would be her kryptonite. Fat chance—but a girl could dream.

Next, her jeans and underwear came off, and the tiny bottom went on. She wiggled the jean shorts on, zipped the fly, and pushed the top button through its hole. If Mom could see her now, she'd faint. Either that or give her a good old-fashioned lecture.

In the floor-length mirror on the closet door, she eyed herself from all angles. There wasn't nearly enough material between her and the world. She watched herself blush, then fled out the door.

She didn't want to think about this. Didn't want to run away. She needed to be brave.… Like her mother would have been—like her friends deserved.

When Olivia entered the kitchen, Stella stood at the island. A jar half full of clear liquid waited on the counter beside two brimming glasses. A white pill lay beside one of the glasses.

"Time to find your joy." Stella picked one glass up and gulped half of it down. Then she held the second glass out to Olivia. "You look white as a ghost underneath your blush. Like an albino with a sunburn. Drink it fast. Otherwise, you might not finish it."

Olivia had never had alcohol before, so she sipped a mouthful. Fumes overwhelmed her nostrils as she swallowed, which threw her into a coughing fit.

Tears of laughter flowed down Stella's face. She pushed the white pill toward Olivia once she got herself under control. "Try not to breathe this time and swallow the pill with your next swig."

Emlyn had told her about the pills, and they'd come up with a plan. Other than an aspirin or two before the collapse, Olivia had never taken any medications. They'd hunted up a penny for her to practice with before she left the house. Now was the true test. She'd better pull it off.

She lifted the pill off the counter, then palmed it as she raised her hand to her mouth. Pretending to toss it in, she held her breath, took another swallow of the liquid, and winced as it burned on the way down.

Stella nodded. "That's enough for now. We need to get going before Nick comes looking for us. Everyone else is already over there."

Olivia slipped the pill into the shorts pocket as she followed Stella. Music emanating from behind Nick's house grew louder as they got closer.

Before they reached the entrance, the gate swung open, and Nick stepped out and closed it. He looked Olivia up and down as his grin grew wider. "Nice to have you join us—finally." He brushed her hair away from her shoulder and slid his finger down the side of her face. "I'm tempted to keep you for myself tonight."

Lead settled in her belly. She had to get into the party. That was the plan.

Please, God, get me past that gate.

"Sounds like our guests are waiting." Stella pulled open the entry to the pool. "You two coming?"

Nick ran his hand through Olivia's hair and rubbed a lock between his fingers. He gave her hair a gentle tug before he released it. "Well, paying guests come first, don't they?"

With a flourish, he waved her toward the pool. "After you."

She released the breath she'd been holding.

The plan was back on track. *Thank you, God.*

23

Chapter Twenty-Three

Inside the fence, Olivia's cheeks heated again. What was worse? To have strangers gawk at you while you're half-dressed, or to have people you know see you in that state? She couldn't be sure, but if her cheeks got any hotter, she'd combust.

A group of men turned when the gate clattered shut behind the newcomers. Nick followed her and shouted to the group. "Don't be shy, gentlemen. These ladies are looking for a good time as much as you are." He winked. "Maybe even more."

Most of the faces were familiar. Caleb, Mr. Worthington, and their neighbors, Mr. Tilbrook, and Mr. Boswell, stood in a semicircle alongside a man she didn't recognize.

Please, God, keep all of us safe.

Nick flicked his hands toward the men. "Mingle, ladies."

She obeyed and felt the slap of Nick's hand on her rear end as she walked away.

This was so humiliating. How did any of the girls do this regularly? She might as well be naked for all the coverage the bikini top provided.

Caleb caught her eye and waved her over. It wasn't as if she didn't know he'd be the one she'd meet up with. After all, they'd walked through the plan dozens of times. But with the alcohol taking effect, her brain felt sluggish.

One foot in front of the other. Slowly. *Don't do something stupid like tripping over your own two feet.* That would be all she needed to happen.

Caleb strode toward her, and they met between the group of men and the gate.

"You okay?" He gripped her waist and pulled her close to whisper. "Whew, I can smell the alcohol. Did you take the drugs?"

The sky spun as she shook her head. "No, just moonshine."

"Put your arms around my waist. I'll keep you steady."

Once she did, he swayed to the beat of the music. He turned them so his back was to Nick, shielding her.

"When… how long…" Wow, she couldn't put her thoughts in order. That moonshine packed a wallop. "Who…"

"Just wait for the signal. Be patient."

Getting drowsy, she closed her eyes and rested her head on Caleb's shoulder. Relaxing into him felt wonderful. This must be what it was like to have someone special in your life—someone trustworthy, solid.

When she opened her eyes again, the men had paired up with the ladies, all swaying to the music.

The current song ended, and another with a faster beat started. The swaying stopped, and she peeked past Caleb's shoulder as the man she didn't know walked up to Nick, pulling Anna behind him.

Anna must have taken something as she was unsteady on her feet. Before they reached Nick, the stranger sat Anna down on a lounger by the pool, then walked the rest of the way to Nick.

Anna's knees knocked together, her feet splayed apart, and her dark hair spilled off the side as she laid down on the reclined chair. At least lying down, she'd be a less likely target.

"Let's move closer to the gate." Caleb's hot breath tickled her ear. "Slowly."

The music continued the fast-paced tempo, so Caleb gyrated while holding onto her hips as their steps inched them closer to Nick and the stranger by the exit. The other couples edged in closer as well. Molly's and Stella's more experienced teasing dance moves took them farther away from their men, then closer. Back and forth.

Now almost beside Nick and the stranger, she saw the stranger hand Nick a wad of cash. Nick's grin grew wider as he fanned the bills. He nodded and waved a hand at Anna.

This was it.

The big sale.

The signal.

"Nicholas Davis." The stranger pulled a gun from underneath his hoodie jacket. "You are under arrest for trafficking of persons for labor or sexual servitude. You have the right to remain silent..."

Nick's eyes bulged, and he stepped back, looking around wildly. He grabbed the closest thing to him—Olivia's arm.

Reeling her in like a chicken about to have her neck snapped, he wrapped his arm around her neck and put her between him and the officer's gun.

Caleb still had her hand, but something sharp pricked her neck. Caleb let go and raised his hands.

"Put the knife down, Nick," the undercover officer said. "We don't want anyone to get hurt. That'll just make it worse."

Nick's arm on her throat was tight—too tight. At first, she tried to free herself. But the knife dug deeper, and a warm trickle ran down her neck. She froze, looking back and forth between Caleb's glare and the cop's insistent but authoritative glower.

Her restricted airway was taking a toll on her ability to think clearly. Or perhaps the alcohol was to blame. Either way, she felt dizzy and took short, quick gasps of air when possible.

Oh God, please help me. I don't want to die.

"You're going to let me out of here if you want her back alive." Nick hauled her backward, toward the gate. "I'd hate to leave her face more tattooed than it already is. But keep coming, and you'll have one less girlie to rescue today."

He continued to pull her backward. As they moved, the knife moved as well. Further away from her neck, then closer—repeatedly with each shuffle toward the exit. One slip too close, and she'd be joining her mother in the great beyond.

They stopped, and Nick growled in her ear. "I can't open the latch on the gate. I'm certain you can understand why. So be a good little girl and reach back to open the gate for us."

She didn't want to obey, but the frustration building on Caleb's face told her all she needed to know. He was helpless to get her out of her predicament. This wasn't in the playbook, no matter how many scenarios they'd gone over.

She reached behind her, thankful to feel the pressure come off her neck slightly as Nick gave her some wiggle room to open the gate.

What she didn't expect was the hand that met hers as she groped for the latch. Small fingers wrapped around hers and gave them a gentle squeeze.

Confusion flooded her brain. Who was behind them?

The fingers released her. Then a feminine voice behind them said, "Hey, Nick."

He spun at the words, and his head met with a brick aimed at his temple. The knife clattered to the ground. Nick followed.

Olivia glimpsed Nadine's face before Olivia fell as well.

24

Chapter Twenty-Four

Olivia awoke in her bed in the pink house. Her throat felt dry and scratchy, and when she lifted her hand to her neck, a bandage stopped her from exploring further. An oversized shirt covered the skimpy clothing.

Her brain jumped back to the shock at seeing Nadine, brick in hand until she dropped it to help Olivia. Though she'd been woozy from the booze, she'd seen Caleb and the officer rush over to handcuff Nick. It hadn't been all that necessary as the strike to his head knocked him senseless.

Her face had been wet, and she realized she'd been crying as Nadine patted her on the back. "You're okay. We're all safe now."

Everything went fuzzy after that.

But why was she back in the pink house? And where was everyone?

She sat up. The room spun and her head throbbed. So, this was what alcohol felt like on the back end. What in the world made Rob want to do this to himself every day?

Once the room stopped its gyrations, she slid her legs over

the side of the bed and got up. Her throat ached for water.

As she padded down the hallway, she heard voices downstairs. Before her foot hit the last stair step, the tones had morphed into the familiar people she'd hoped would be there.

"Well, look who's up," Caleb said as she entered the kitchen. "Come on in. You're the hero of the day."

All the men from the pool party were there, except for the officer. She didn't see any of the girls, but Mrs. Worthington had joined the group.

Emlyn was also there and ran over, flinging her arms around her. "I was so worried about you." She brushed against her bandage, then backed off, and guided her to sit on one of the stools. "Does it hurt? Are you okay? What do you need?"

"I'm fine." The words croaked past Olivia's tongue, which seemed swollen and stuck in her pasty mouth. She cleared her throat and tried again. "I just need a drink of water—thirsty."

Mrs. Worthington dashed to the cabinet to get a glass, then had it filled, and held it out to Olivia within seconds. "How do you feel, dear? You were so brave."

She accepted the glass and gulped it down. When Mrs. Worthington stretched her hand out for the empty glass, refilled it, and gave it back, Olivia sipped. "Thank you. Where did everyone go?"

Mr. Worthington spoke first. "Nick is on his way to jail with Officer Bradley. Nadine went with them as she had quite the story to tell. She wanted to be certain it was all documented."

Olivia couldn't shake the image of Nadine holding the brick. "She saved me."

Mrs. Worthington nodded. "From what she says, Nick bought her when she was just sixteen, before the collapse occurred. She's been with him ever since, but never thought she could leave until she realized what you'd done. As soon as she figured out the party was a setup, she knew it was her way out."

An involuntary shudder ran through Olivia at the thought of one person owning another. That had to have been why Nadine had tried so hard to dissuade her from coming to the pink house. It also explained her sour moods.

But what about... "Where are the other girls? Anna, Brandy—"

"They're fine." Clapping, Emlyn bounced over and wiggled up to sit on the island before her. "Carissa took them to her place for the night. Molly and Stella couldn't believe men out there wanted to rescue them, instead of use them. Anna was out of it from some pills she'd taken, but Brandy wanted to see the bees."

Relief rushed through Olivia. They'd done it. They'd emptied the pink house of all the girls Nick exploited, and he was behind bars. Her plan had worked, but no way would it have without everyone's help.

Then another question came to her, and shivers skittered over her spine. Almost afraid to ask, she clutched Emlyn's hand. "Does anyone know what happened to Lilly and Ruby?"

Her friend's lips tightened, and her jaw jutted up. "Nadine told Officer Bradley what she knew. Nick sold them. The details are sketchy, and so far, Nick isn't talking."

Olivia's stomach ached. She'd been too late. Tears welled in her eyes, and the sympathetic faces surrounding her made the pain worse.

"You saved everyone else." Caleb knelt in front of her. He placed a hand on hers. "If you hadn't come to us when you did, who knows how much longer Anna and Brandy would have been around? Nick offered to sell them to us. If the wrong person had come along first, they'd be gone too."

Knowing he was right should have helped. But… she'd won the battle and still lost the war.

"Why don't you stay with us tonight?" Mrs. Worthington offered. "The other girls are safe with Carissa, especially with Nick in jail. You're both welcome to stay as long as you like."

How tempting to accept the offer—to let someone else take care of her for a while. She felt like an emotional rag doll someone had tossed on the floor. Then she saw Emlyn, her best friend, and knew she wasn't alone.

"Thanks so much for the offer, Mrs. Worthington." She pulled Emlyn to her side. "We're good at the house. We've got a chicken to take care of and wood to split for market day. We're going to be fine."

They would be too. They had friends they could rely upon if needed. They were going to contribute to the community, just like the rest of their neighbors.

"How about I come over tomorrow and help with some of that wood splitting?" Caleb gave her the cutest smile she'd ever seen. "Not that you can't handle it, but perhaps a few pointers to get you started?"

Now that was her kind of neighborly love.

25

Chapter Twenty-Five

Not everyone liked winter, but it was one of the best times of the year, especially now that they'd built back up their chicken flock. Though the garden grew slower in the winter, the cabbage and broccoli were coming along. Olivia was determined to learn to cook Brussels sprouts the way Mrs. Worthington did. They actually tasted good instead of mushy and disgusting. If she could master the task, they'd plant those next year.

She'd settled into her bed, exhausted after a long day of wood splitting. A smile crept over her face in the dark of her room. Caleb seemed to show up every day lately to make sure they were all using safety precautions. Today, he'd invited her out on their first official date.

It wasn't like they could go to the movies or a restaurant, though she hoped those simple pleasures would be around again someday. Who knew, perhaps her children would have time to be creative? They may be the first postapocalyptics to publish a book, produce a movie, or write a play for the entertainment of others. For now, all efforts still went to survival.

It would come, though. Someday technology would return… supply chains humming along once more.

Until then, it would have to be the simple pleasures of life—maybe a picnic. He'd mentioned a friend who raised horses, so he might take her to look at them. The Worthingtons talked about purchasing a pair to pull a wagon back and forth on market day. They'd all be living like the Amish soon if things didn't turn around. After all, cars didn't last forever when there weren't spare parts to fix them.

The house was quiet, except for a whispered conversation farther down the hallway. Giggles followed as if it were a teenage slumber party. Laughter was her favorite sound these days—because of who made the sounds.

It had taken a while to track them down, but Officer Bradley led the team that pulled Ruby and Lilly out of their imprisonment in a basement. Days after the team rescued them in Atlanta, they moved home to Shiloh. Tonight, they shared secrets. The snickers told her the confidences were innocent, though—not the stuff of nightmares.

Emlyn had taken over Rob's bedroom. She'd also become an expert at driving the wedge into the logs to split them. Today's strenuous work fine-tuned her biceps and sent her to bed early. Exhausted sleep left her room silent.

Molly and Stella stayed with Carissa, as did Anna and Brandy. Together, they were building the property into an even larger farm. Now that Carissa's house was full, she negotiated a good price on the land next to hers, and the group had plans for a spring garden on the plot.

Hours later, Olivia had just nodded off when something startled her awake. It was dark out the bedroom window. The front door thudded closed. Who would have gone outside at this time of night?

She sat up, listening.

People whispered in the kitchen—male voices, *strangers* in the house.

Caleb had offered to show her how to shoot and wanted her to keep a gun by the bedside. Why had she said no?

She knew why. No way could she put a bullet into another human's body.

She clenched her fists. Too bad she didn't have one now. At least it would look threatening.

What should she do? Was it possible one of Nick's former customers figured out where the girls had moved? The thought of someone being after Emlyn, Ruby, or Lilly made her blood boil.

No one was touching her friends again.

Moonlight revealed the shadows of her room's contents. Her lamp was the closest object. But the porcelain base wouldn't do much damage.

What about Rob's bat? Where had she last seen it? Probably in his bedroom closet.

The voices were still in the kitchen. There'd been no power tonight, so they couldn't turn the lights on. She was just grateful the power company put a moratorium on billing for what little power there was. Otherwise, they'd never have any. She slipped out of bed and tiptoed to her door. The voices had moved to the living room. They'd be heading toward the bedrooms next. She needed to hurry.

Easing the door open, she stepped into the hallway, padded to the next door, turned the knob, and slipped into the room.

Wham! She was body-slammed to the floor.

Oomph. The colliding weight knocked the air out of her lungs.

"I've got a gun," a voice whispered in her ear. "If you as much as twitch a muscle, I'll use it."

She froze, taking a beat to regain her breath. As soon as she could, she hissed back. "Emlyn… it's me, Olivia."

Arms reached out to her. "I'm so sorry," Emlyn whispered, louder this time. "I thought you were a home invader."

A light shone on them, and they both squinted into the beam, unable to see who held it.

"Olivia? What are you doing on the floor? And who's this?" Uncle Kevin inquired.

The beam revealed a second person in the hallway—Aunt Amanda standing there, holding a backpack. "We're home?"

The light lifted to show Rob standing behind Uncle Kevin with a goofy grin. "Hey! Long time no see."

Both girls scrambled to their feet as the bedroom door down the hall opened. "Olivia? That you?"

Lilly and Ruby joined the family gathering in the hallway.

"Who are these people?" Uncle Kevin spread out his hands. "We're in the right house, aren't we?"

"I'm fine with guests." Rob's grin grew wider as he rocked back on his heels, taking in the view down the hallway. "I can sleep on the couch."

Aunt Amanda gathered Olivia into her arms. "I'm glad you made it back home. We were worried about you."

She had so many questions, but the first one on her tongue was a private matter.

Placing her hand on her aunt's, she pointed toward the front of the house. "Let's go out to the porch and chat, okay?" Then she held out her hands to her friends. "We're going to be tight now. Emlyn, can you move into my bedroom? Ruby, Lilly, since Rob's offered to take the couch, you can share his room for the rest of the night."

As she guided her aunt toward the kitchen, everyone returned to their bedrooms to get resituated for the night. Rob offered to help them move items, but the girls could get them on their own. After many all-night girl chats, Olivia knew they had difficulty trusting men, even those they knew.

Rob would have an uphill battle to make friends with this crew.

Once Olivia and Aunt Amanda rested on the porch swing, Rob and Uncle Kevin followed them outside so the family was alone together for the first time in months.

Olivia started the conversation. "I didn't know if I'd ever see you all again. My friends needed a safe place, so I invited them to stay with me here. We can all share my room now that you're back."

Uncle Kevin nodded. "I'm sure we can convert the game room into another bedroom. We'll figure it out."

"You look good." Aunt Amanda looked her up and down. "Better than when we left. So, you're doing well."

"We've been cutting wood with Caleb's help." She tangled her fingers with Aunt Amanda's and squeezed, then smiled at Rob, who seemed alert and interested. "Also raising chickens, growing crops—and I'll have bees this spring." The thought alone gave her a buzz.

Rob rubbed the back of his neck and scuffled his shoes. "I need to apologize, Olivia. What I did to you was so wrong. I messed up."

A gentleness softened some of her remaining rough edges. He was different now, back to the prealcohol version of Rob.

But what if he returned to his old ways? How could she ask him about his drinking without sounding negative? She wanted to trust him—but she didn't. He didn't need to hear that, though.

He raked a hand through his longish hair. "I've been sober for a month now. I was on and off a bit before that. If Mom and Dad hadn't taken me to Atlanta when they did, I'd be dead."

After looking first at his father, then his mother, he let his gaze rest on Olivia. "I've already had plenty of time to apologize to them, and they've forgiven me."

He moved over to stand by the swing where she sat. "I'm glad to hear Caleb has been helping you. He's a good guy, and I owe him—and probably half the neighborhood—an apology. And I promise they'll get it." He gazed around him before refocusing on her. "I know I need to prove to you I'll stay sober. I'm determined to make it right between you and me. And Caleb."

He held his hand out to her. "Will you give me a chance to try?"

Though part of her wanted to stay angry, his clear eyes and obvious remorse gave her all the proof she needed for today. He meant what he said.

She jumped off the swing, threw her arms around his waist, and gave him an enormous bear hug. "Welcome back, coz."

The End

* * *

Dear reader, thank you so much for sharing Olivia's journey with me! If you enjoyed reading *Collapse: The Death of Independence*, I would gratefully appreciate you leaving a review on Bookbub, Goodreads, or other sites to help others discover my books. Those minutes of your time make a tremendous difference to writers like me, not only in helping others find our books but also in encouraging us to keep up the effort of writing.

I'd love to have you join *my* posse of friends! Join my newsletter at www.AngelaDShelton.com and receive a **free** copy of my novella *Collapse: Downfall*. You can also connect with me on Facebook, Instagram, Medium, and Pinterest.

See you next time!
Angela

About the Author

Angela D. Shelton works as a healthcare accountant and owns/works a cattle ranch in Georgia.

Calling on her experience from the ranch and drawing on her husband's military and law enforcement understanding, she's created a post-apocalyptic world in her novel series, **Collapse**. The stories revolve around a small-town Georgia family who turn to farming just in the nick of time to be self-sufficient when the supply chains in the world collapse.

Ms. Shelton is a member of the Christian Indie Publishing Association, the American Christian Fiction Writers, and Word Weavers International.

You can connect with me on:
 https://www.angeladshelton.com
 https://www.facebook.com/AngelaDShelton.Author

Subscribe to my newsletter:

✉ https://landing.mailerlite.com/webforms/landing/b7g1g6